JOHNNY APOCALYPSE

BOOK 1:
Johnny Apocalypse
and the Nuclear Wasteland

BOOK 2:
Johnny Apocalypse
and the Fight for a New World

BOOK 3:
Johnny Apocalypse
and the Battle for Freedom

BOOK 4:
Johnny Apocalypse
and the King of New York

Join the Johnny Apocalypse Discord:

ymBcADDZFR

JOHNNY APOCALYPSE

AND THE KING OF NEW YORK

MARK ROBIJN

BLUE FORGE PRESS

Port Orchard, Washington

Johnny Apocalypse and the King of New York
Copyright 2022
By Mark Robijn

First eBook Edition July 2022
First Print Edition July 2022

ISBN 978-1-59092-865-3

Blue Forge Press is the print division of the volunteer-run, federal 501(c)3 nonprofit company, Blue Legacy, founded in 1989 and dedicated to bringing light to the shadows and voice to the silence. We strive to empower storytellers across all walks of life with our four divisions: Blue Forge Press, Blue Forge Films, Blue Forge Gaming, and Blue Forge Records. Find out more at www.MyBlueLegacy.org

Blue Forge Press
7419 Ebbert Drive Southeast
Port Orchard, Washington 98367
blueforgepress@gmail.com
360-550-2071 ph.txt

Dedicated to all the Johnny Apocalypse fans out there who kept asking, "When's the next Johnny adventure coming out?" You inspired me with your love of Johnny to keep writing. I hope you find Johnny's new adventures thrilling and exciting.

Thank you!

ACKNOWLEDGEMENTS

I would like to acknowledge the invaluable inspiration I received from some of my favorite authors who inspired me to write the Johnny Apocalypse adventures, including:

I am Legend by Richard Matheson
The Berserker Wars by Fred Saberhagen
The Martian Chronicles by Ray Bradbury
Call of the Wild by Jack London
The Lord of the Rings by J. R.R. Tolkien
The Stand by Stephen King
Planet of the Apes by Pierre Boulle
The Hunger Games by Suzanne Collins

JOHNNY APOCALYPSE

AND THE KING OF NEW YORK

MARK ROBIJN

PROLOGUE

One hundred years after the Mushroom Monsters fell, the world is a tattered fabric of destroyed cities, rusted old cars and broken remnants of a society long departed. Vegetation has grown over everything, giving the whole world a look of dense, moldy forest. Beasties roam the land, dog-beasties and cat-beasties, and others much more dangerous. Wildies, half-crazy wanderers trying to scrape out a living in the barren wasteland, also fill the cities. Gangers roam the cities as well, cutthroats and pirates looking to prey on the weak, or alone. New societies and new monsters have been created out of death and destruction. This is the time of Johnny Apocalypse.

Johnny Apocalypse, his tribe, and their new friends have won their battle against the Doomsday Prophecy and Lord Algon, and so, have earned a time of peace and rest. Now they spend their days getting to know their new allies and settling into their new Sanctuary in the old city of Washington Deecee. Work goes on to build a stable and safe society based on the ideas of democracy and freedom, as Misterwizard has taught them. But Johnny has made his intentions to head off on his own for new adventures. He wants to see more of the world that has been sheltered from him for his whole life. And so, Johnny and his friends prepare to leave New Sanctuary, his tribe's new home, and set out on the road to see what new adventures awaits them.

CHAPTER 1

On a warm spring day when the red eye rode high in the sky and warmed the land, Johnny met with Misterwizard in the new building he'd claimed as his new castle. Even though it was made of red brick and not white stone like Misterwizard's old castle, it still somehow reminded Johnny of it because it was tall and elegant and hade a huge dome at the top. It was just a few blocks away from the big lawn where the Captol and New Sanctuary were. From the outside, it looked to Johnny like a bunch of square blocks stuck together, all different heights and going in different directions. Still, it was an impressive building that looked important.

Inside, it seemed even larger and more impressive than Misterwizard's old castle, for there was one huge room with a marble floor and in the middle, you could see inside the dome which soared up into the air.

When Johnny walked inside for the first time, he just stood and just gazed around, especially at the walls.

Beautiful paintings and stone people covered them, and long, tall pink columns went from the floor all the way to the ceiling. There was a white statue of some women holding a man who looked like he was dying in her arms, and Johnny wondered who he was and who had killed him.

Right in the middle of the room, Johnny could look up and see the inside of the dome. The red eye from outside shone on the colored panels of the dome to make entrancing colors all over the walls.

Misterwizard told Johnny the name of it, but it was strange, something like, 'catedol of sant matew' or something like that. It was one of the funniest phrases Johnny could ever remember Misterwizard saying, and he didn't even try to remember it or figure out what it meant. He just knew that he liked it almost more than Misterwizard's old castle, for it seemed even more elegant and mysterious than the old one.

Misterwizard already begun to make it like his old castle and fill it with wonderful objects from the world before that he had painstakingly restored. He had taken out the wooden benches that had filled the place and now strange metal contraptions filled the room, along with more old cars Misterwizard was busy fixing and fake people wearing strange, colorful clothing.

White stone statues of people mostly staring off into space, paintings of people just sitting and looking at Johnny, cabinets with strange looking devices in them that long ago ceased to serve any function, suits of shiny steel armor and frail looking stick furniture filled every room. It was almost like being back home again.

In a large room up a set of stairs to the right of the main hall, Misterwizard had made himself another bedroom and workroom. In it there was a large four-poster bed and huge fireplace with a fire that crackled merrily. Misterwizard was back to his tinkering and experimenting, and had a big map on the wall and piles of books all over the floor. In the corner of this room there sat a huge, red comfy looking chair. Next to it Misterwizard had a table, and on that table, he had his cigars, a box of chocolates and a bottle of red liquid Misterwizard called "wine."

Misterwizard sat there now smoking a cigar and enjoying a glass of wine as he talked to Johnny, who stood gazing at the big map on the wall. Misterwizard was a short round man, with a bald head and a happy smile. He always reminded Johnny of a funny creature Johnny had once seen on a poster that Misterwizard called a "minion." Misterwizard always seemed full of energy and pep, bouncing from one task to another, despite his round size, and Johnny had yet to find him not busy doing something.

Misterwizard spoke. "I must be totally transparent with you Johnny; I am going to miss you and your friends exponentially and I don't say that in an esoteric way. I will find myself in extreme distress until I find you and your companions once again in my presence."

Johnny, dressed in his usual leather vest, leather pants and big boots, his short yellow hair uncombed and sticking up in all directions as it always did, moved over and sat in another chair on the other side of the table, one with wooden arms, a velvet seat and a straight back that Johnny didn't find comfortable at all. He did have a table next to him with some of Misterwizard's chocolates, and a cup of something Misterwizard made for him that was delicious, what Misterwizard called "hot chocolate." And once again, he couldn't understand half of what Misterwizard said, but he was used to it.

"We'll miss you too, Misterwizard. I promise we won't be gone long. Deb and Super are already saying how much they're going to miss their parents. They've never been away from their home before. But then, neither have Starbucks and I."

Misterwizard took his cigar out of his mouth and waved it around, making smoke circles in the air. "Posh and pernicious. Neither you nor I have developed the skill of precognition my friend, and so there is no way to satisfactory predict the moment of your reintegration into the tribe. But, if we are to honestly consider the logical necessities, your journey is actually inevitable. We must discover what has become of America if we are to reunite it. However, I appreciate your familial intentions to make your trip a brief one."

"What's a logical necessities?" Johnny asked, taking a sip of his hot chocolate. It was actually very good and he smiled, thinking how he was going to miss Misterwizard's fine cooking while he was gone.

"It means that the task you are endeavoring upon is something that has to be completed, and the sooner the more beneficial. You see Johnny, if we are to restore the Republic, we need to know the current sociology of the inhabitants. We need to know what other tribes and indigenous groups have sprung up under the unique and never before occurring reimaging of the state of the planet."

"Indigi—" Johnny's head started to hurt from the effort of trying to figure out the fancy words.

Misterwizard bounded up and strode to his map, puffing hard on his cigar. Johnny stood up and hurried to follow.

When they both stood before the map, Misterwizard took his cigar out and used it to point. "This is a linear representation of the land masses on our planet, Johnny. Unless there has been some seismic activity, I suspect it is just the same as it was before the Great War."

Misterwizard turned to Johnny. "However, the social and societal groupings have no doubt undergone a complete metamorphosis. Ergo, it is a world totally unrepresentative of the one that existed previously.

"And," a shadow crossed Mistewizard's face, "we

have no prior data on what the amount of radiation that has inundated this planet will cause. Some cities were undoubtedly totally destroyed, laid waste, and others have only the mild effects of ancillary radiation. Still, there may be strange physiological changes in both men and beasts that have hitherto never occurred."

Misterwizard turned and smiled impishly at Johnny. "In other words, you may find not only men, but monsters and mermaids."

Johnny grinned back and just nodded. Misterwizard had totally lost him again.

"Johnny, I need you to do reconnaissance. Just like Lewis and Clark you must explore the land and make copious notes. Find out who now inhabits our land. What tribes and gangs, what fauna and flora, what strange beings now roam the land? What is their philosophy and governmental affiliation? What rules govern their society and dictates their actions? You must ferret this out and report back to me, so we can understand the challenges ahead to rebuilding our nation."

"You want me to—"

"Explore! Find out who is out there, how are they living, and how willing they might be to join us."

Misterwizard pointed with his cigar to a dot on the map. "And here is a good place to start. It is called, 'New York.' It used to be a bustling town, one of the largest in the country. Millions used to live there, and in my wanderings, I observed a large tribe living there that seemed fairly organized. Go see what kind of society has sprung up since the Great War there. And maybe take in a show."

"Take in a show?"

"Go forth and explore!"

"We'll do it, Misterwizard!" Johnny said, taking a swig of his hot chocolate.

Misterwizard approached him with a look of caution. "Be careful though, Johnny. There may be tribes and creatures abroad who will not welcome you. Try to remain unobserved, unless it is absolutely imperative that you make contact. I want to see you and your friends back safe and sound to New Sanctuary."

"I will Misterwizard. We can be really quiet if we need to be."

"Good! Remember all I told you about the country before the mushroom monsters. We must restore what was good in our society once again, the tenets of democracy, freedom and life, liberty and the pursuit of happiness for all! We must reinstate the inalienable truths that all men are created equal, and we must reinstitute the Constitution and the Bill of Rights as soon as possible, before more egregious and nefarious forms of government take hold. We must restore the United States!"

Johnny just nodded, not understand most of what Misterwizard said, as usual.

Then Misterwizard paused and looked at Johnny,

seeming to be deep in thought. Johnny wondered what he was thinking. Then he spoke.

"You are now sixteen seasons, Johnny. Due to the improbability of survival past the age of thirty in your old society, this was chosen as the time when you will become a man. It also means you are able to select a mate."

A rush of love filled Johnny's heart as he realized what Misterwizard was talking about. Johnny nodded his throat tight with emotion.

"I know. I've thought about it a lot."

Misterwizard put a gentle hand on Johnny's arm. "And of course, you've chosen your fair maiden Deb as your lifelong companion."

Johnny breathed in deeply. "If she'll have me. I can't believe it's really going to happen, Misterwizard. I'm really going to get to be with Deb, forever."

Misterwizard felt emotion beginning to overtake him as well, so he straightened up his short little frame and cleared his throat. "No better man, Johnny. None at all."

Misterwizard smiled and they hugged. "Go slowly, come back quickly, my good friend," Misterwizard said as he patted Johnny on the arm. Johnny nodded, suddenly full of sadness to be leaving at all.

Then Johnny did leave, and Misterwizard pretended to be poring over his books, but Johnny caught him looking up, his face full of sorrow at seeing Johnny go.

As Johnny left Misterwizard puttering around and puffing on his cigar, he walked out of the big red brick building. He gazed back at it with pleasure, and wondered how long it would be before he was back again. The afternoon red eye warmed his body as soon as he walked out, and he enjoyed the wonderful feeling for a moment, trying to get his feelings at leaving Misterwizard and his thoughts of his love for Deb under control.

Then he looked up and his mouth opened wide with surprise, for a whole crowd of people stood waiting for him. There before him on his right stood Deb and her parents Thegap and Bathandbodyworks, and Johnny's parents Foodcourt and Teavanna. Standing off to Johnny's left stood Super and her parents Crownroyal and Liptontea and Starbucks and his parents, Barnesandnoble and Liztaylor.

Johnny was instantly curious to see them all gathered together like they were, and he wondered if something was wrong. Had something new happened?

"What's going on?" Johnny asked, looking at Starbucks, who smiled back at him with a strange look of emotion.

Starbuck's father, a tall, strong black man with wide shoulders, a big nose and a penetrating gaze, stepped forward. Johnny turned to him with a quizzical look. "Johnny, we're all here because Deb and Super's parents have something they want to say to you and Starbucks before you leave on your great adventure." He turned towards Thegap, who smiled then stepped forward too.

They all wore happy smiles, which made Johnny even more curious to know what was going on.

"Johnny," Thegap said, "you know we have always said we gave you our blessing in choosing Deb as your mate."

Suddenly Bathandbodyworks, Deb's mother and the ugliest woman Johnny had ever seen, burst into tears and took out a piece of cloth. She dabbed at her eyes which had begun to water. Super's mother and father looked overcome as well, and Liptontea, Super's mother, with black hair just like her daughter, also looked like she might cry at any moment.

Thegap went on. "Now, you and Starbucks plan on taking our daughters with you on this big adventure. We are fine with this, but first we feel it is only right that you and our daughters complete the Ceremony of Choosing and truly become mated before you go, to make things proper."

"My poor baby!" Bathandbodyworks wailed, and

she blubbered into her cloth.

Once again, Johnny's chest filled with emotion, and it irritated him, not wanting to appear weak and unmanly, but there was nothing he could do to stop it. He gazed at Deb. She smiled back at him shyly, and he could tell she was filled with emotion as well. Her eyes were moist and looked as if she might cry too.

Starbucks gazed at Super and held her hand. Super looked shy and reserved, not like her at all.

"That is," Liptontea said, "if you boys really want to have our daughters."

Johnny tried to control the tightness in his throat and the emotions that threatened to spill out on his face. He walked over and took Deb's hands. They smiled into each other's eyes.

"It's what I've waited for, for years," Johnny said.

Then tears did come to Deb's eyes. Her lips trembled and Johnny took her into his arms and held her close.

"You know we love your daughters more than anything in the whole world," Starbucks said, as he put an arm around Super. "We want to spend our whole lives with them. That is, if they want to."

Super's lip trembled and she looked weepy. She tried to brush it off with one of her usual jokes. "Sure, what else do we have to do?"

Everyone chuckled, all overcome with feelings.

"Fine!" Crownroyal, Super's father said. "We'll

have the ceremony in front of the whole tribe! Back at our old Sanctuary this was one of the few happy occasions we got to enjoy. This time we are going to make it a really big deal. It will be wonderful!"

"My poor baby!" Bathandbodyworks wailed again. Everyone else couldn't help but chuckle.

Johnny gazed into Deb's eyes. "Is this what you really want, Deb?"

Deb smiled, and for an answer, she reached up and gave Johnny a kiss. "Don't you remember anything? I told you, where Johnny goes, I go."

Johnny kissed her again, this time so long the others began to feel a little awkward, so they began breaking up.

The parents talked to each other in happy tones and slowly walked way. Johnny, Starbucks, Deb and Super watched them leave.

"This is it," Super said. "We're really grown-ups now."

"Yep," Starbucks said. "It's about time for you."

Super punched him in the arm, and they all laughed. Then Starbucks and Super walked back to New Sanctuary too.

Johnny turned to Deb. She walked over to him and took his hands. They gazed into each other's eyes, both thinking about what they were about to do, but both too shy to speak.

Johnny put his arms around Deb and she wrapped

her arms around his waist. They began to walk back.

"After this, we'll be leaving. Are you sure you're okay with that?"

Deb put her head on his chest and smiled. "How many times to I have to tell you…"

"I know. Where Johnny goes, so does Deb. I just want to make sure you're not just doing it because I want to."

Deb turned and took Johnny's chin in her hand. "I love having adventures with you, Johnny. I want to see the world, just as much as you do. Why would I want to stay here, when there's so much to explore?

Johnny took her hand off his chin and kissed it. "How did I ever find a girl so wonderful, so perfect for me?"

"Oh, Johnny," Deb said, her eyes moist. "You could have had any girl in the tribe. I'm just glad you picked me."

They kissed again, pressing their lips together, feeling the soft touch of each other's skin and touching each other's bodies. Johnny put his hand in Deb's long blond hair and felt its soft, velvet touch. The world fell away as they kissed and enjoyed knowing that they would always be together.

One red eye cycle later, it was all prepared. They waited until the red eye was down over the hills and night approached so the Undergrounders would feel comfortable attending. Wildies went through the long and tedious effort of moving their tents and shacks back on the lawn so there was a nice big space for the ceremony, though it took them a lot of work.

Since it was spring in Washington Deecee, a wonderful thing had happened that no one expected or knew was coming. The trees that lined the lawn and dotted the landscape, those that had not been destroyed during the fight with the gangers, had begun to spout little pink flowers, and they blossomed everywhere. The scrabblers loved to climb the trees and shake the branches to make the flowers fall. Then they would adorn their hair and their houses with them.

Now the people of Sanctuary, still divided into their three separate groups of the Tribe, the Wildies and the Underdgrounders, all sat on the lawn waiting for the big event to begin. Misterwizard had made a special treat he called "cake" for the occasion, as well as some of his now famous spagetta, but it had all been eaten long ago, and not everyone got some. Now they all just sat, some chewing on food they'd brought from their own homes, others merely dozing, waiting for something to happen.

With the backdrop of the crumbling ruins of the tower that had once been the Washington monument, the pink flowers were laid to make a big ring on the grass. Other different flowers had been found also, some yellow ones and red ones, and they were strewn all over the lawn and placed just about everywhere to be seen, on steps of the buildings and even adorning some of the wildies' shacks.

At the front of the large ring stood Misterwizard. He wore a huge grin and looked immensely pleased. He held a black book that he always used when he officiated a pairing ceremony. No one knew much about it, for it had lots of funny words in fancy letters that even Misterwizard didn't understand many of, but it looked important and magical and it had colorful pictures of strange scenes.

Misterwizard wore a black suit he had found in the old building once called the Museum of American History that had once been worn by a man named "Lincoln." It really didn't fit his short, round body and he had to roll up the legs and arms and pin them. The jacket went down to his knees and he looked like a big, black penguin-beastie. He had a black top hat on his head that had also belonged to "Lincoln," but it was too big too and kept slipping down over his bald head, blinding him. He finally decided to take it off and set it on the grass next to him.

The parents of the teens all sat in chairs at the edge of the circle, the only ones with them, and they had all tried to clean up and look as fancy as they could, though most of them only had one or two sets of clothes.

On one side of the circle, Misterwizard had rolled out big, black wooden box on three legs. It had a strange row of white and black sticks all lined up on one side that looked like teeth, and a top that opened to reveal strange yellow metal strings inside. Some of the teeth were missing, and some of the strings as well, and one of the wooden legs was braced with a metal pole.

In front of the teeth of the box on a black four-footed stool sat Abercrombie, Sephie's mother, her round, squat body positioned in the middle and legs so short they didn't touch the grass. She had practiced all night to play the strange teeth, and now she pounded on them with both hands. Sometimes when she touched one of the teeth nothing would happen, but other times, a warbled ringing would sound, clunky and hollow. The sound was pleasant at times and other times just loud, but she kept slamming the teeth with a big smile and wild abandon, thoroughly enjoying herself.

In the middle of the circle stood Johnny and Deb and Starbucks and Super, holding hands. Johnny wore his usual outfit, his leather pants, boots and vest over a white shirt, with his sword and slingshot on his hips, but he had taken care to clean his clothes as best he could.

Deb however, looked like an angel in a long white dress Misterwizard had found her. It was yellowed from age and had a black stain on the back, but she still looked radiant in it as she gazed at Johnny with love. Her long blond hair cascaded down the back but was covered with a white veil, and she looked beautiful.

Starbucks looked fancy in long black pants a dark red shirt and a long black jacket he'd found, all of which looked elegant against his dark black skin. Super wore jeans a white shirt and a jean jacket, not one to try to impress anyone. She had put flowers in her black hair though, and makeup on her face she'd found, though not being used to using it she used a little too much and her lips, eyelashes and cheeks were dark red.

Abercrombie continued to bang away at the keys until Misterwizard loudly cleared his throat. When that didn't get her attention, he frowned and spoke in a loud voice.

"Thank you, Abercrombie, for the melodious and totally enrapturing…"

She didn't hear him, lost in the pleasure of banging the wooden teeth, swaying back and forth.

Misterwizard spoke louder. *"Thank you, Abercrombie, for the most delightful…"*

She still didn't hear, and people began to look at each other and laugh.

"Cease and desist, woman!"

Finally, Abercrombie heard him and she raised her hands and looked towards him, slightly embarrassed.

Misterwizard grinned again and turned to look at Johnny, Deb, Super and Starbucks. He smiled with pleasure and motioned them forward. Johnny and Deb gazed at each other, and so did Starbucks and Super. They all stepped up to stand before Misterwizard.

Misterwizard raised his hand, and everyone quieted down. Then he looked into his magic book.

"In the beginning, God created the heavens and the Earth. And the Earth was without form, and void."

The audience listened intently, not understanding a word of what he was saying, but knowing it was something magical and important.

Misterwizard turned to another page. "Do not speak to fools, for they will scorn your prudent words."

The people sat quietly, not sure what they should think or what they were supposed to do. Misterwizard turned to another page and peered into the book.

"I will climb the palm tree, and take hold of its fruit."

Everyone looked confused, even Johnny, Deb, Starbucks and Super. Misterwizard frowned and closed the book. He set it on a table behind him, turned to the crowd and smiled.

"Now, now, now. We have finally arrived at this most satisfactory and long anticipated event, for which I at least have waited for what seems like a millennium, though as we know time is relative when you are impatient for a specific moment to arrive."

Deb's mother burst into wailing, and soon Super's mother joined her. Everyone looked at them and chuckled. Foodcourt, Johnny's dad, looked proud. He wore a yellow suit and shirt and looked like a giant banana. He put his arm around Teavana, Johnny's mother, who wore a blue dress with one sleeve missing and gave her a squeeze.

Misterwizard turned to the teens. "Johnny Apocalypse, Little Debbie, Starbucks and Superfragilisticexpialadocious, please step forward."

Johnny and Deb and Starbucks and Super all laughed, stood up and walked to stand before Misterwizard, holding each other's hands.

Misterwizard turned to Johnny. "Johnny, you have chosen Little Debbie as your mate, to join you throughout all of your adventures, to cherish and love until some unpredictable twist of fate ends one of your lives or more pleasantly, old age causes one of you to expire before the other. No matter was terrors and dangers you both face, no matter hardship or starvation or pestilence or fire, no matter how much you disagree and bicker over mundane and unimportant issues, you will face life together, fighting valiantly at each other's side. If this is your desire Johnny, please acknowledge in the affirmative."

Johnny turned and gazed into Deb's eyes. She smiled back with love and happiness. "I sure do."

A cheer went up from the crowd, and Deb's mother wailed even louder.

Misterwizard turned to Deb. "Little Debbie, in similarity, you too have chosen to make Johnny Apocalypse your mate, to fight by his side, to tend to his wounds, to cheer him up should he fall into the pit of despair, to correct him should he wander into folly, and to die, if need be, by his side. Is that correct?"

Deb looked up into Johnny's eyes. "Forever and forever!"

Now more of the women in the crowd were weeping, and some of the men had wet eyes too.

"Then you are hereby mated, for all time. Don't try to get out of it, for it's too late! Johnny, you may, uh…"

But Johnny was already ahead of Misterwizard. He kissed Deb and she kissed him back, their eyes closed, lost in each other's touch.

Misterwizard smiled with joy and waited for Johnny and Deb to finish. Everyone watched and laughed, but after it appeared that they weren't going to stop for a while, Misterwizard cleared his throat and turned to Starbucks and Super.

"Starbucks…"

"Enough speeches!" Super yelled impatiently. "We do!"

Starbucks and Super kissed, and everyone cheered.

Misterwizard chuckled. "Well, then, that's over! Let's start the party!"

Everyone jumped up laughing and talking. The teens' parents ran forward to congratulate them, and the scene turned into one of happy chaos.

When the yellow eye was high in the sky and the stars peppered the dark blue night, Johnny and Deb spent their first night together. Misterwizard had prepared a special room for them in the White House. Though part of the building was destroyed, there were at least two bedrooms still intact. The one he chose for Johnny and Deb was called the Queen's Bedroom, and it was beautifully furnished with a large four-poster bed and mirrors.

As Deb sang to herself in the bedroom, Johnny, uncharacteristically shy, sat on the end of the bed in his regular clothes, feeling a strange new kind of fright that he didn't recognize, one that seemed to make him feel embarrassed and all tied up in knots inside.

Deb walked into the room, combing her long blond hair, a flower still above her ear. She smiled at Johnny with affection, and he felt his heart fill with quiet joy and gladness. She wore a black silk thing Misterwizard have given her as a gift he called a kimono.

She walked over and sat next to Johnny. He turned to her and took her hands.

"Maybe tonight, Johnny will find a reason to take his clothes off, for once."

Johnny and Deb both laughed. Johnny kissed her and held her close, and very quickly they were lost in the throes of passion.

Nearby in another room, it was Super who was uncharacteristically shy. She puttered around the bathroom of what had once been the Lincoln Bedroom. Starbucks lay on the bed, impatiently waiting for her, staring at the bathroom door.

"Are you almost done in there?"

"Any time now," Super said.

Starbucks rolled his eyes. Then he grinned. He hopped up, went to the bathroom and opened the door. Super turned and looked at him, and he could tell she was a little afraid.

He walked over to her and took her hands. She giggled, and he kissed her. Then she swept her up into his arms as she yelped and carried her into the bedroom as they both laughed.

In the morning, they rose packed food and supplies on their Harleys, said goodbye to their friends and family, and with Deecee along in the basket of Johnny's Harley, they rode off into the distant sunrise.

CHAPTER 2

The red eye peeked over the far horizon, shining its golden light on the broken buildings, reflecting off the few windows still intact. It brightened the empty streets and rusted cars of Washington Deecee. Vegetation covered every surface, over the cars and on the streets, making the city seem like a jungle.

Smoke rose from fires still burning, reminders of the recent battle between Johnny's tribe and the Gangers. For a city that appeared so empty, there was life everywhere, stirring again after a long slumber.

A quiet filled the air, as if the world waited for some signal to come to life. That signal came in the form of an ear-shattering roar of a Harley speeding down the moss- covered street, and then a second right behind it. Even though it was early, not everyone slept, certainly not Johnny, his girlfriend Deb or their friends Starbucks and Super. And definitely not Johnny's dog-beastie, Deecee. They had woken early to start their long trek to destinations unknown.

The sound of the engines echoed off the empty buildings and rusted cars and hung in the still air, as if not wanting to disappear. Some of the sound was absorbed by the lichen and moss trying to reclaim the city. A rabbit-beastie sitting in the grass by the side of an abandoned playground in the square open area in front of a building stopped eating and looked up, instantly alert for danger. The sound grew and grew, until it seemed to fill the whole World. Then the strangest sight the rabbit-beastie had ever seen came speeding up over the nearby hill. The rabbit-beastie stared at this new oddity for a moment before hopping off in the opposite direction for safety.

Johnny and his friends did look like quite a sight. Johnny, a white boy of sixteen seasons with short yellow hair, would have looked handsome and rugged in his black leather jacket, black leather pants and black boots, if it weren't for the funny goggles over his eyes. Deb, his girlfriend, now mate, also sixteen seasons, sat behind him, holding on, her long blond hair flowing down the back of the black leather jacket Johnny found for her. She wore jeans and a pair of purple cowboy boots Johnny gave her as a present. And next to them in his own special seat sat Deecee, a handsome, big black dog-beastie with a splash of white on his nose and chest that in the old days would have been called a "Siberian Husky," wearing goggles of his own that made him look even more comical.

Behind them on his own Harley rode Starbucks, a black boy of seventeen seasons, in a jean jacket festooned with patches that looked cool but meant nothing to the boy wearing them, and Super, his sixteen-season old white girlfriend, now mate, with long black hair, an elegant big nose that came from her Italian heritage, though she had no way of knowing it, and dark eyes. Super wore a tee-shirt and a red sweatshirt with the picture of a mouse-beastie in yellow pants and white shoes on it, a pair of jeans and some ratty looking pink tennis shoes.

Johnny stopped his Harley at the top of the hill, and Starbucks did too. Johnny took off his goggles and looked down at the city. Deb, Starbucks and Super turned to look at it too. Deecee barked.

Johnny looked at Deb, and saw she gazed back at the city, looking melancholy.

"This is it, Little Debbie. If you go any further after this…"

Deb laughed and squeezed Johnny's middle, then put her head on his back.

"I told you—"

Johnny started to finish the phrase when Starbucks and Super joined in. "Where Johnny goes, I go."

"Shut up!" Deb said, grinning. Deb gazed down at the city. "It's just all happening so fast. We were in Sanctuary, and then we were free in the big world, and before we could even enjoy it, we were running for our lives from the Gangers. I was sick, and didn't know much that was happening, and then we were in that big fight. And we met such interesting, strange creatures, and saw those amazing metal monsters. And now that we finally have a new home, we're leaving again before we've had a chance to really catch our breath."

Johnny, Starbucks and Super looked at her, thinking about what she said.

Johnny studied her face. "If you don't want to go, we can go back, stay for a while."

Deb shook her head. "No. I want to go. I want to see the whole world with you, Johnny. But you can understand if I have some feelings about it, can't you?"

"Sure," Johnny said. He and Deb held each other and touched cheeks.

"I agree," Super said. "I am going to miss everyone too." She looked at Johnny. "But not as much as I'm going to enjoy getting away from them for a while. I think you guys know what I mean. How long are we going to be gone, Johnny?"

"Not too long," Johnny said. "We'll start out with a nice short ride and then come back to see how everyone's doing. How does that sound?"

"Sure," said Starbucks. "We'll be back before they even have time to miss us!"

Deecee barked again. Deb found one of the special bones Misterwizard had packed just for Deecee and held one up to him. Deecee grabbed it in his mouth with delight, sat down in his seat and chewed it.

They all smiled and nodded. "That sounds like a good plan," Super said. "Everyone in favor?" They all raised their hands. Deecee, as if not to be left out, barked.

Starbucks revved his engine, making them all smile. "So, where are we going on this adventure, Johnny?"

Johnny smiled and started his Harley again. "I thought we'd go back and visit Misterwizard's castle again where we can get more special water for our Harleys, then our old Sanctuary, then… we'll just do what Misterwizard said. "

"What did he say?" Deb asked.

"Play it by ear! Whatever that means."

They all laughed, excited to start their adventure.

Then Johnny took off. Deb laughed and held on,

putting her head on Johnny's back again. Starbucks and Super grinned, looked at each other and shook their heads. Then he started up his bike and sped up to follow.

Far behind them, a lone figure watched them from inside a beat-up car parked behind an old rusted bus, just far enough out so the driver could see. With no hood and dents all over, the car was painted with skulls and bright colored pictures of knives and bombs. Before the Great War it had been a Lincoln Town car, but time and weather had turned it into nothing but an orange rusted steel hulk with wheels. Still, someone in the Doomsday Prophecy, Ripper's gang had fixed it up enough so it drove, and that was all that mattered.

In the driver's seat, so large that he barely fit, was a man, over six feet tall and big and wide like a walking mountain. He wore a black leather jacket that was too small for him so his arms stuck out. His long, black hair, matted and dirty, clung to his head. He had a long beard that made him look like the old pirate Blackbeard. That, along his dead eyes and the scars that he had all over his face, down his chin, over his left eye and between his eyes across his nose, made him look like a walking corpse.

He also sported burn scars on his neck and down the whole right side of his body from when he'd been too close to an explosion during the Gangers' fight with the Tribe, the skin red and wrinkled.

On seat next to him he had a stash of weapons, a wicked looking curved sword, a large hammer, an old-fashioned revolver and a sharpened stick. He stared at Johnny and his friends with his good eye filled with pure hatred.

"You think you're free now Johnny. You killed Ripper. You killed Leaker. You kill all the Doomsday Prophecy. But not Monsta. Monsta was hurt, but not dead. Monsta is going to get revenge for everybody. He will crush Johnny's skull with his bare hands while Johnny's girl watches and screams. Then he will take Johnny's girl and make her Monsta's. Ripper will see from the grave and smile, proud of Monsta."

When Johnny took off, Monsta drove off as well, smiling darkly, following them slowly so as not to be seen.

From a side street, unseen by Monsta and not knowing he was there, another stranger also followed Johnny. This was a woman, with long blond hair on one side of her head and the other half shaved. On the bare side of her head, a tattoo of a red skull was emblazoned.

She wore a black leather jacket and black gloves with spikes. Her name was Lady Stabs, and she was a friend of Johnny's and the Tribe's. She rode a Harley she'd found so she could be just like Johnny and Starbucks. She watched them leave with a look of longing, as if she wished she could join them.

Lady Stabs knew she shouldn't follow Johnny and Starbucks, and if they found out, they would be mad at her for spying on them. But she owed Johnny so much, she had decided she would follow them, always at a distance alone, a protector to help them if they got into too much trouble. She didn't care if she was alone for the rest of her life, following them across the land. She had no one, and her life wasn't that valuable anyway. She owed Johnny her life, and she wanted to pay him back, somehow.

As Johnny and his friends took off, she waited for a few seconds to put some distance between them, then with a turn of the throttle, she roared her engine and took off, following just close enough so as not to lose them, but far enough away that they wouldn't hear her or spot her.

CHAPTER 3

Johnny and Starbucks sped on and soon left Washington Deecee far behind. The gray road, full of holes and old rusted cars curved past overgrown trees and collapsed houses. Even though they were not in the city there were still buildings and houses along the road, all looking deserted. In the distance to the left between the buildings they saw open fields and blue skies. The red eye shone down hot, making their backs sweat.

Large trees with big red leaves also lined the road, sometimes mixed in with the trees with pink flowers, and other trees too. Some of them had begun to grow right in the street, and Johnny and Starbucks had to weave around them to keep going.

Some of the cars still held skeletons, though they were so old and faded they didn't even look real. Every once in a while, one of the travelers would see something, like a bird-beastie in the sky, a strange, interesting building or a wildie and then point at it and shout, trying to be heard over the roar of the engines. They had to slow down often to avoid the giant cracks in the road and the broken-down rusted hulks of cars, and a few times they had to stop altogether, for the road was completely blocked. Then they'd have to try and lift the Harleys over the old cars to continue on.

Johnny and his friends drove and drove, putting miles behind them. Deb fell asleep on Johnny's back. The wind whistled through their hair and the red eye beat down on their backs, making them all sleepy. The city of Washington Deecee soon became just a mirage on the horizon behind them, and then disappeared altogether.

Suddenly Johnny stopped, making Starbucks stop as well. Deb woke up to see what had happened. She saw Johnny, Starbucks and Super simply sitting there, staring ahead. She looked to see what they were looking at, and smiled with curiosity.

There in front of them stood a whole herd of some kind of beastie. The creatures simply stood there, staring back at them, not attempting to move.

"What are they, Johnny?" Starbucks asked.

"Are they dangerous?" Super asked.

"I don't know, but I think they're called, "cow-beasties.""

"Why are they staring at us?" Deb asked, not fully awake. "Are they going to attack?"

The cow-beasties just stood there, staring, chewing on something.

"Well, they're in our way," Super said grumpily. "Scare them away."

"I don't know," Johnny said warily. "I don't want to make them mad."

"What do we do, Johnny?' Starbucks said.

"Let's just try and go around them, really quiet like."

Johnny started his engine, but didn't rev it. He moved forward as slowly as quietly as he could and tried to drive around the large herd. He had to go completely off the road and into the grass.

Deecee barked and looked like he was about to jump out.

"Grab Deecee! Don't let him attack them!"

Deb grabbed Deecee's collar, keeping her eyes on the herd of cow-beasties.

Suddenly the whole herd, spooked by Deecee's bark took off thundering in the opposite direction. Johnny and his friends laughed, watching them.

"They don't look to dangerous to me," Starbucks said, grinning. "They look more scared of us then we are of them!"

"Let Deecee go! Let him chase them!" Super said.

"Do you want to be the one to find him again?" Johnny said.

"Uh, nope," Super said, laughing.

When the herd was off the road, Johnny turned his bike and drove back on it again.

"I think those are what people used to eat, in the old days," Deb said.

"I think you're right," Johnny said. "We should remember this spot and tell Misterwizard about them. We might need to capture them and bring them to New Sanctuary for food."

They all watched the cow-beasties until they were out of sight. Then they all smiled at each other and turned back to watch the road.

A few minutes behind them, Monsta stopped and stared at the cow-beasties with a look of hunger. He saw one in the road ahead of him, and grinned. He gunned his engine and headed straight for it. The cow-beastie ran, but it was no match for the large car, and with a thud Monsta hit it. The cow-beastie fell to the pavement. Monsta stopped, got out and walked over to it. Taking out his knife, he knelt down and cut its throat. Then he laughed.

"Ripper would like that I bet. I'll show you what Ripper would do."

He cut through the cow-beastie's tough hide and sliced down through its middle. Pulling out organs, he kept going until he found the heart. Then he cut it out and held it high in the air. With a look of savagery, he bit into it, blood dripping down his chin.

He grinned and chewed on it, gazing around at the empty world, blood dripping from his mouth onto his beard. Then suddenly he started crying. He wept, his head bobbing up and down. He beat the ground with his fist. Then he wiped his eyes.

"You killed them all, Johnny. You killed my friends. You're gonna pay. I'm gonna eat your heart too!"

He wiped his eyes with the back of his bloody hand, smearing more blood on his face, and cut a big slab of meat off the dead cow-beastie. Then throwing it over his shoulder, heedless of the blood dripping down his jacket, the walked back to the car and threw the meat in the trunk. He left the rest of the cow-beastie and climbed back in his car and drove off, still chewing on the cow-beastie's heart.

"Someday, I start up the Doomsday Prophecy again. After I kill Johnny. Then all of his people will pay. I'll eat all their hearts!" He drove off again in pursuit of Johnny.

A few seconds later Lady Stabs passed the dead cow-beastie and stopped long enough to look at it. Did

Johnny and his friends do that, she wondered? It didn't seem like something Johnny would do. But if they were hungry enough, maybe they had no choice. She shrugged and drove on, looking down at the grisly sight one more time with disgust.

When the red eye was high in the middle of the sky, Johnny saw an old abandoned house with a big, tall tree next to it with some inviting shade. He pulled over under the tree and stopped so they could have lunch. Far behind them, the car stopped and pulled over. And behind it, the stranger on the bike also slowed and finally stopped. Lady Stabs saw Monsta now, but she didn't know who he was, and wondered why he too followed Johnny. She watched to see what the person in the car was going to do.

As Johnny and his friends got off the Harleys, they all stretched and looked around. There were other houses nearby and on the other side of the gray ribbon of highway, and behind them beyond the house they could see what looked like a small town. Johnny and Starbucks started unpacking the saddle bags from their bikes that held their lunch. Deecee jumped out of his seat, ran around in a circle and then stopped next to Johnny so watch.

Deb looked at the empty, forlorn house behind them. Its door was open, and the inside looked dark and sinister. The windows in the front of the house were gone, the glass in piles on the porch. Deb could see inside that grass had started to grow not just up around the house, but was growing up through the floorboards as well.

"Is that what people used to live in, Johnny?"

They all looked at the house. Deecee looked up at too. He sniffed and looked suspicious.

"I think so," Johnny said. It was something he had never talked about with Misterwizard. "I think they had much smaller tribes back then."

"Do you think one family lived in each one?" Super asked. "Or maybe two or three. Or maybe each man made his own tribe."

"Don't be silly," Starbucks said. "They were all one big tribe, right Johnny?"

Johnny frowned, wishing they'd stop asking him questions he didn't know the answer to, because it made him look silly. "Sort of."

Super slugged Starbucks in the arm. "Ow!" He yelled, grabbed his arm and glared at her.

"Don't call me 'silly,' whatever that means. I'm going to explore it."

Super strode off towards the house.

"Hey, wait for me! Who's going to protect you?"

Super turned and gave him an angry look. "Are

you trying to get me to punch you in the nose?"

Johnny and Deb laughed as Starbucks took off after Super with Deecee tagging along. Johnny and Deb were alone. Deb walked over and grabbed Johnny's hand. Johnny, who had been busy putting out sandwiches on a blanket in the grass, stopped and turned to gaze at her.

Suddenly Deb kissed Johnny, and he kissed her back. They were instantly both lost in the sensations of each other's touch and feel.

Deb stopped and put her arms around Johnny.

"Johnny, I didn't know life could be so wonderful. It feels like we've just finally been born, after being asleep forever."

Johnny held her close and put his chin against her head. "This is just the beginning, Deb. We're going to have a whole new world to build."

Starbucks, Super and Deecee came back, and Johnny and Deb parted. Starbucks saw what they were doing and grinned.

"You want us to leave for a little longer?"

They all laughed. "No," Johnny said. "I'm hungry, let's eat. What did you see?"

"Nothing but a bunch of moldy rooms overgrown with weeds and dirt," Super said. "There were old pictures on the walls so faded you couldn't see what they showed."

"There were some old dirty lumps in the first room that I think were something you once sat on," Starbucks said, making a face. "But they are so gross, I wouldn't want to, now."

"There was lots of stuff that looked like the kind Misterwizard says runs on 'lectricy,'" Super said. "One had some letters on it."

"What were they, Starbucks?"

"It looked like X, B, O, X." Starbucks said. "What does that spell, Johnny?"

Johnny shrugged, and tried to think what the letters could spell, but they didn't form any words he could remember.

"Doesn't look like a very nice place to live. But I did find this." Super held up a piece of paper. They all come over and stared at it. On the paper, there appeared to be a family, a man, a woman and two children, though the paper was faded to be almost white.

"Look, they must have lived before the Great War."

"I wonder if they survived, and their children are alive today," Deb said.

"Probably not," Johnny said, somberly.

Down the highway, the old car sat, and the man watched them. He chewed on cow-beastie heart, blood and goo covering his face. He glared at Johnny and his friends and growled deeply in his throat. "Any time. Just wait 'till you make a mistake. Nobody to protect you out here, Johnny."

Johnny and his friends finished their small lunch of sandwiches, apples and water Misterwizard had packed for them and then got back on their Harleys. Soon they were speeding off down the road, followed by their unknown pursuers.

Suddenly in the distance, a huge city appeared on the horizon. But there were only a few buildings that were just shells, empty skeletons, and the ground around them looked flat and covered with rubble.

"Wow," Johnny said over the sound of the engines. "That place looks even worse than Pill-a-delpa. It must have been visited by one of the Mushroom Monsters."

"Yeah," Starbucks said. There isn't anything left!"

"What city is that?" Super yelled.

Johnny slowed down and stopped and Starbucks pulled up next to him.

"I don't know," Johnny said. "We passed through it on the way to Washington Deecee, but we didn't stop. It seemed deserted and worthless."

"I don't remember it," Deb said.

"You were sleeping most of the way," Starbucks

laughed. "You probably don't remember much of anything."

They came to a signpost on the side of the road, leaning crazily and half-melted. Johnny stopped and looked up at it.

"What does it say, Johnny?" Deb asked.

"We-cum to Ball-tim-moree," Johnny sounded out the letters, the way Misterwizard taught him, talking slowly with a serious look of concentration.

"Ball-tim-moree?" Starbucks laughed. "That's even funnier than Pill-a-delpa."

They all gazed at the city in front of them. The noon red eye shone down on the empty streets. What buildings were left only had bricks over the bottom half, and rubble filled the streets, covering the rusted hulks of the cars.

Johnny smiled, remembering his days in Pill-a-delpia, exploring on his own. "This is it! Our first city to explore together."

The rest all smiled too with anticipation. "Yippee!" said Deb. "We never did get to do much of that with you before."

"What do you think we'll find?" Starbucks asked excitedly.

"Who knows?" Starbucks said, grinning. "Weapons, or gold, or more strange gadgets like

Misterwizard is always finding."

"Yay!" yelled Super.

"We'll have to keep an eye out for beasties, wildies, and gangers," Johnny said.

Suddenly Deb's gaze turned somber. "Do you really think we can make a new world out this this, Johnny? It all seems so empty, and dangerous, and destroyed."

Johnny put an arm around her. "It will take time, but someday, I hope we'll be 'Merica again. But this time, we won't mess it up with mushroom monsters."

"What are we talking for?" Starbucks said. "Lead the way, Johnny!"

Johnny took off again and Starbucks followed, traveling down a major street that led them under the sign and to an area with flattened buildings and rusted shapes that were so distorted it was hard to even tell they were once cars.

They drove down the street, staring at the empty buildings and the massive destruction all around them. It seemed so desolate and bare. Not a creature moved, and no bird-beasties sang. Nothing seemed alive for miles, as if they were looking at a painting instead the real world. Johnny looked for any buildings that might look interesting or have something in them, but most looked so barren and broken down they didn't look promising.

Suddenly from inside the remnants of a building, a figure stepped out. It stood on four legs and had four arms with no hands. Its head was a shapeless dome, with only black eyes with no lids, a ragged hole for a nose and a ragged mouth showing sharp, pointed teeth inside. It was strange and hideous.

Its whole body and head were black, and it looked like a giant black spider-beastie. It had no neck, its head just melted into its shoulders. All down the arms and legs were strange round fleshy discs. It wore no clothing.

Johnny and Starbucks were moving so fast, they passed by the figure quickly, and only Deb and Supers saw it.

"Eeek!" Super yelled, pointing. "Starbucks, look!"

"Did you see that?" Deb added. "It was hideous!"

Johnny turned his head to answer. "See what?"

"That thing!" Super said. "Talk about freaky!"

"It was horrible!" Deb added.

"Just another Wildie," Starbucks cut in, though he hadn't seen it.

"I hope there's not more like that," Deb said. "He looked really scary!"

"Here we go, Deb," Super said, looking not too happy, at Deb on the Harley ahead. "Starting our next adventure."

"I'm not ready!" Deb said, turning her head back

to look back at Super. Then she looked at Johnny. "I thought you said this place was deserted!"

"It is," Johnny said, not understanding what she was talking about. He shrugged and kept on going.

Soon they were in the middle of the city. Tall buildings surrounded them, most broken and twisted, but still making them feel small and vulnerable. Most were so empty they could see all the way through the windows to the other side. Only a rare few of the windows still had glass in them, and the glass was dirty and discolored. Here because of the devastation, it was taking the vegetation longer to grow back, so everything just looked barren and dirty, piles of rock and rubble.

Johnny stopped in the middle of one block. The red eye shone down on the barren landscape. On either side of him, tall jagged buildings soared into the sky. Old rusted cars sat on either side of them, round lumps really, and an old bus lay on its side in the middle of the street, its tires and seats long gone, only the metal still remaining. The day was hot, and the travelers gazed around, enjoying the sights. Still, Deb and Super were nervous, looking for more strange creatures like the one they'd seen.

"What it must have been like, when this place was full of people, and they lived in these tall things going way up to the sky," Starbucks said.

"Can we go up inside one, all the way to the top?" Super asked, smiling darkly.

"Are you crazy?" Starbucks said. "We don't even know how to, and we might get trapped inside."

"Cowardie!" Super said, and slugged his arm. "How high have you been in one, Johnny?" she asked, leaning to the side so she could see Johnny's face.

Johnny thought about it, and felt a little ashamed that in all his adventures in Pill-a-delpa, he'd never had the courage to go up more than a few levels. "Not very far," he replied, sounding casual. "I didn't see any reason to."

"Besides," Deb said, "there might be more of those terrifying creatures around."

"What creatures?" Johnny asked.

"Hello, the slimy creatures with four arms and four legs!" Deb said.

Johnny looked at her to see if she was joking, but she looked serious, in fact she looked worried. Johnny looked at Super and she wasn't smiling either. He shrugged and decided to be extra cautious.

Suddenly a strange warbled scream filled the air. It was shrill and sharp and instantly hurt their ears.

"There's more now!" Deb pointed, her voice rising in panic.

At the other end of the street, a horde of black

creatures too many to count, barreled towards them on their four strange legs like spider-beasties, looking terrifying. Worse yet, they all held huge clubs or crude swords. Their mouths were open in wicked-looking grimaces, showing pointed, sharp teeth. Their dark black eyes boiled with anger.

"Johnny, go!" Deb yelled, gripping his shoulders hard and accidently digging into him with her fingers.

"Starbucks, get us out of here!" Super screamed.

"You bet I will!" Starbucks yelled, as both he and Johnny hurried to do just that.

CHAPTER 4

"**W**ow!" Starbucks said, turning his Harley as fast as he could to follow Johnny, who took off in a squeal of tires. Behind them the screeching of the creatures filled the air and made their hearts beat fast.

"They're almost on top of us!" Super yelled as she looked over her shoulder behind them. The creatures were fast and before the adventurers could get very far, they were already at the end of the block just behind them. Johnny and his friends could see the monster's faces twisted with terrifying grimaces. Their black eyes glistened with menace.

"That doesn't look like the Welcome Wagon!" Starbucks yelled as he wove around the rusted remnant of a car.

"Ooh, they are gross!" Super said. "What are they?"

"They're not like us, that's for sure," Deb said

"Looks like they're looking for their next meal!" Johnny yelled as he drove along a large crack in the street. He had to go around it for the road on the other side was higher where the street had buckled. Deecee watched the creatures from his seat, growled then barked, but even he sounded a little afraid.

"They're so fast!" Deb yelled, for even though they pushed the Harleys as fast as they could go, the creatures still seemed to be keeping up with them, even getting closer.

"I've changed my mind! I don't want any more adventures!" Super yelled, hanging on for dear life.

They reached the middle of downtown Ball-tim-moree and tall buildings surrounded them on all sides, dark and empty, like giant tombs. As they passed a cross street Johnny looked to his left. More of the creatures, a whole pack of them ran towards them. Johnny looked to his right. Another group!

"Johnny, look!" Deb said, pointed towards the group to their left.

"And look over there!" Super said, pointed to the mob heading towards them on the right.

"And look ahead!" Starbucks said, his voice rising in panic.

As Johnny looked in front of them, he saw the

street was filled with more of the giant black monsters. They were trapped!

"There's no place like home, there's no place like home!" Starbucks yelled.

Despite the danger, they all grinned at Starbucks.

"What does that mean, Dummy?" Super said, hitting him on the shoulder with her fist.

"It's something Misterwizard said when he was trapped by the Gangers. They are magical words to help you escape!"

"Well, let's hope they work!" Johnny said with a grin. "Follow me!" He turned his Harley towards the towering building on his right. The windows of the building had all been smashed out, and they could see all the way to the other side through the holes left behind.

Johnny bounced up the stone steps leading to the entrance and Deb squeaked. Starbucks followed, and just in time. The black monsters chasing them reached the street, and the others from all the other directions joined them.

Johnny sped towards the opening of the building. The front of the first floor had once all been glass but the glass was all gone, shattered, as were the glass doors, leaving only the stone pillars holding the building up. Johnny roared his bike inside and drove down a hallway to four sets of closed double doors.

Starbucks sped in right after him. They both slowed and turned their bikes around. Outside, the black monsters filled the square. The friends could hear the creatures screeching at each other in high-pitched squeals. Then the creatures all turned towards the building. They ran towards it. The friends were trapped inside!

"Well, I guess we're going up whether we like it or not!" Johnny said. He hopped off his Harley and pulled Deb off.

"I changed my mind too," Deb said. "I don't want to go exploring anymore!"

The friends looked around. Johnny saw a door with the same word on it that the door to the stairs at Misterwizard's castle had, "Stairway." He ran towards it. "Follow me!"

The rest didn't need a second invitation. Running to the door, Johnny turned the handle and pushed. Outside, they could hear the screeches of the monsters approaching.

The door didn't budge!

"Help me, Starbucks!"

Starbucks came over and together he and Johnny smashed their shoulders against the door. Finally, it banged open. All four adventurers hurried past it into the dark, cool space beyond.

Lady Stabs rode into the empty, lonely city, secretly yelling at herself. She'd stopped for a bite to eat and to take a little nap, and now she'd lost Johnny and his friends. She had no idea where they went, and she was really worried she'd never find them again. And there was someone else following them, who Lady Stabs didn't know was a friend or foe. If she couldn't find them again, she'd have to either go on searching forever, or go back home, feeling like a total loser and a louse-beastie for letting Johnny and his friends down.

The tall buildings towered into the sky, like silent sentinels, and she felt all alone. Once again, she wished she could join Johnny and his friends, for it was lonely riding around all by herself, and probably dangerous too. If something happened to her, no one would even know. She thought to herself, *And would anyone really care?* She stubbornly put that thought away. Maybe when she was a member of the Death Prophecy no one cared, but now she was a part of the Tribe, and she had real friends. She decided that she would prove it. When she found Johnny and his friends again, she'd tell them she was following them. They would surely invite her to join them, and that would prove to her that somebody cared.

Looking forward to this moment, she smiled and rode on, past rusted old cars and the skeletons of the people from before. Even though the red eye was high in the sky, a breeze still blew bits of paper and tumbleweeds down the street. The wind felt good on her face, cooling it, and she looked down each street she passed for Johnny and his friends.

She saw something strange and slowed down. It was something black and huge. She didn't stop, for she suspected whatever she was looking at wasn't friendly. As she motored past as quietly as she could, she kept an eye on whatever it was.

Then suddenly, the thing turned and Lady Stabs saw it. It was a huge, hideous creature with four black legs and four arms! It chewed on what looked like a deer-beastie, holding it with both hands, chomping down with relish. Lady Stabs had never seen such a horrible looking thing before. It was as big as the rusted cars and twice as tall.

The monster saw her, and its eyes filled with fury. Lady Stabs gunned her engine and sped away, leaving the monster to stare after her.

What was that? she thought. Once again, she felt vulnerable and alone. If there were more of those things, and they surrounded her... maybe she wasn't as courageous as Johnny. Maybe she was being foolish going out all by herself into the weird, strange world that now existed.

Suddenly she heard loud, painful screeches ahead. She slowed down again, not sure where to go. She decided to creep forward, just close enough to see what was going on but still far enough away to escape.

What she saw filled her with amazement and fright. A hundred of the same black monsters stood in front of a building, screeching and shaking swords and clubs. It looked like they had someone trapped, and whoever it was, they were in big trouble. Could it be Johnny and his friends?

Monsta drove his rusted, beat-up car into the dead city. The sound of its engine coughing and sputtering echoed through the empty rubble-filled streets, creating a lot of noise, which worried him. Monsta didn't like being trapped in city among the rusted cars and the tall, dark buildings. He had lost track of Johnny, which meant he could drive right past him without knowing. Then Johnny might see him first, and his element of surprise would be gone. He decided he'd have to drive really slowly, and try to make as little noise as possible. He slowed down and peered out the holes where the windows in his car had once been. Just to pass the time, he grabbed another hunk of the deer-beastie meat and chewed on it, though he really wasn't hungry any more.

He passed an old rotted bus with the top gone and saw something strange inside. Stopping for a second, he listened. He was sure he heard the sound of high-pitched snoring. He stopped his car, got out and walked over to the bus. He peered inside. There was a monster sleeping in the middle of the bus!

Monsta gazed at it and tried to figure out how big it was. Monsta was big, but nothing like this thing. Its head was near the front of the bus and its four arms lay splayed over the wire mesh that was left of the seats. It was so tall its four legs were near the back. It seemed to fill up the whole inside of the bus!

Monsta thought to himself, *What a good ally this creature would make to fight Johnny.* He wondered what he could give it to make it join him, or if he could even talk to it. He knew that Ripper was really the one good at thinking up things like that, and in his mind, he cursed Johnny again for killing him. What would Ripper do? He tried to think. He would offer them something. To join the gang, that was it! But would this thing want to join the gang for? It might not even be human. Then he remembered, there was no more gang, and he cursed Johnny again.

Food! He could offer it food! Or funny water! The stuff you drank that made your mind go silly. Or dames! He could offer it dames! The thing was, he doubted the creature would want any of those things, and it could probably get them for itself if it did.

What do you offer a giant black monster to make it want to fight you? He had it! He would tell them about Johnny's tribe! Surely this creature would consider Johnny's tribe a good food source.

He smiled and walked over to the door of the bus to introduce himself.

CHAPTER 5

ohnny, Deb and their friends started up the stairway in the pitch-black darkness. It was so dark it felt like a slime coating them, sucking the courage out of their hearts and filling them with fear. They could hear each other's footsteps and breathing, labored and sounding scared. Deecee, cowed into silence, padded quietly next to Johnny, his fur rubbing comfortingly against Deb's leg.

Deb clung to Johnny's hand with her right hand and waved the other one in front of herself, afraid she was going to fall. She felt around until she found the railing and grabbed it. It helped her feel some sense of reality, took away the feeling of being lost in a giant void.

"Man," Starbucks said, his voice echoing in the darkness. "I thought we faced some crazy stuff before, but this is even weirder!"

Johnny chuckled. Starbucks was sure right. If this

was the kind of things he and Misterwizard would face in the new world, it was going to be quite an adventure trying to get Merica going again.

Super spoke, and her sudden words in the darkness, somehow seeming loud, made Deb's heart jump. "How far are we going?"

As if reading everyone's thoughts, Starbucks said, "Shhh!"

"Why?" Super said grumpily, her voice a floating apparition in the darkness. "No one's here."

As if in response to her, a sudden thumping came from the door below. The monsters were at the door, trying to get in.

Deecee whined in the darkness.

"It's okay, Boy. We better keep going, for a while," Johnny said, somehow sounding strange in the dark.

"How will we know when we're at a door?" Deb said, sounding woozy, as if the dark was affecting her. "We can't see anything!"

"And how will we know if something is here to attack us?" Super trilled, her voice rising with fright.

"I'll feel the wall when we get to the next flat place," Johnny said, his voice sounding confused too. "If I feel a door, I'll open it, just to get some light."

"I hope so," Starbucks said. "I don't think we can

stand too much time like this, or we're going to go wildie."

Just then, a shout came from way above them, somewhere in the dark. It came from a man, and it sounded crazy, like a wildie. It sounded distant, as if it was miles away, and they couldn't make out what was said. Instantly they all froze in fright. Deecee barked in response.

"Shh, Deecee!" Johnny scolded.

Their breathing sounded heavy in the darkness as they all stood, waiting to see if the voice came again. It did, but it didn't sound like the person was addressing them, just yelling. Still, it gave them all the shudders. "Let's take the next door!" Starbucks said.

"I agree!" Super said.

"Okay, try to hurry but watch your step," Johnny replied.

They reached the next flat space and stopped.

"Stand still, nobody move." Johnny whispered. "I'll look for a door."

Deb felt Johnny let go of her hand, and suddenly she felt totally alone, lost in a sea of darkness. She reached for and found Deecee's back. She kept her hand on it, feeling his nice, soft warmth. Still, she felt like any moment she was going to trip and fall all the way back down the stairs, screaming through the air. She grabbed

Deecee's fur and waited unhappily for Johnny to return.

Suddenly light burst upon Deb, Starbucks and Super, hurting their eyes after the darkness and making them have to close them. Johnny had found a door!

Bright light streamed in, and when they opened their eyes again. they could see they the stairs going down, and another set going up. Above the door, it said "Mezzanine," whatever that meant. Deb, Starbucks and Super hurried through the door, overjoyed to leave the creepy darkness.

Lady Stabs peeked around the corner of a building across the street from where the black monsters gathered. She had dismounted her bike and it sat a few feet behind her, pointed the other direction, ready for a quick getaway.

The strange black creatures seemed very excited about something. As she watched, a huge black one, bigger than the rest, looking as big as an old bus, strode through the crowd. The others all parted to let him pass, and Lady Stabs instantly understood this was the creatures' leader. It wore gold bands on its arms and a big gold necklace on its neck. It had strange symbols carved into its flesh. It looked even more menacing than the rest.

It strode to the front of the crowd. One of the other monsters crawled up to it and pointed at the building with one of its arms. Then it screeched something that made Lady Stab's ears hurt.

The monster waved its arm around as it screeched, pointing at the street with another arm and at the building with another, as if describing something going inside.

The black monster leader's eyes narrowed and it spoke, but this time it was quieter and slower, in a high-pitched voice.

The monsters all raised their weapons and screeched, and Lady Stabs knew whoever they were after was in big trouble.

Then she saw someone inside on the second floor. There were four people there. With dread, she realized who the four people were. It was Johnny and his friends, and they were trapped, surrounded by big, black monsters.

As Monsta peered in the door of the bus, he realized who the real monster was. He was called Monsta, but this creature was the real thing. He could hear the giant creature snore, a wheezing, high-pitched, inhuman sound. Something about the creature made his skin crawl. Now that he was about to wake it up, he began to have serious doubts about how smart a plan it was. The creature might just grab him and eat him. Monsta was big, but this thing was twice as big, and he was pretty certain it was not even human. He would be no match for it. He decided to leave it alone, maybe find another way to use the creature without actually talking to it. He slowly turned to leave, as quietly as he could.

Suddenly Monsta heard a loud bark. He turned and looked. Near the corner of a one-story building with a big yellow "M" on the side he saw a pack of the meanest looking dog-beasties he'd ever seen. One, the leader, was big and black with pointed ears and a long, lean face. Next to it stood a gray, mangy dog with matted fur and its fur in its eyes. On the other side stood a short but bulky one, brown and white, with a pushed in face. They all stared at Monsta, and he knew they wanted him for their next meal.

In a flash the dog-beasties took off towards him. Monsta knew he could take one of them, maybe two, but not the whole pack. He looked for his car and saw it was too far away, he'd never make it. He made a quick decision and climbed into the bus.

As the dog-beasties snarled and barked outside, Monsta carefully and as quietly as he could tip-toed past the sleeping monster. He made it halfway through the bus when the first dog-beasties climbed inside. It was the big, black leader.

The dog-beastie stopped just inside while the others waited outside, barking and snarling. It surveyed the bus, looking cautiously at the sleeping monster, then back at Monsta. Deciding Monsta was the smaller and safer prey, it padded past the giant towards Monsta, silent and with menacing eyes.

One of the monster's black eyes opened. It saw the dog-beastie and raised its head. Monsta smiled, for the dog-beastie seemed to know this giant was nothing to mess with. It turned and ran towards the door again.

But the creature was faster. It screeched and reached out a black tentacle. It grabbed the dog-beastie. The dog-beastie yelped in fear and then snarled and bit the giant's arm. But as Monsta watched in horrid fascination, the creature opened its mouth wide, showing rows of sharp, jagged teeth. With a chomp it bit down on the dog-beastie and tore a section out of its middle. The dog-beastie howled in pain then went silent as the giant creature chewed, the dog-beastie's blood dripping down its chin.

Monsta felt his insides turn to gel and he felt like

throwing up, but part of him was excited and cheered by the gory scene. But Monsta knew he was in real danger, for if the creature saw him, he would be next on the menu.

Fortunately for Monsta the giant creature was intent on eating the dog-beastie. It continued taking bites out of it as it rose up and walked out of the bus. From the windows, Monsta saw the other dog-beasties surround it, snarling and barking.

Monsta knew he was in for a show, and he slowly crept to the back of the bus to make his get-away, keeping his eye on the drama happening outside.

As Monsta watched in grim pleasure, the dog-beasties took turns scampering in and nipping at the giant creature, looking for a weakness. The black monster threw the dead dog-beastie in its hand away and turned in a circle, trying to keep all the dog-beasties in its sight at once. The dog-beasties looked hungry, hungry enough to even take on the monster, and the it roared at them in fury.

A huge dog-beastie leapt in and bit the monster on one of its back legs. The monster screamed in pain and beat at it. Another dog-beastie snuck in and bit one of the monster's front legs. Monsta began to wonder if he was going to see the dog-beasties take the monster down and eat it.

But Monsta forgot the creature had four arms. Just as he began to think the monster was losing, it grabbed a dog-beastie and held it in the air. At the same time, it grabbed another of the dog-beasties, who yelped in fear. As Monsta watched in amazed delight, the creature flung the smaller dog-beastie through the air. It sailed off into the distance to finally smash into the side of a building. Then as Monsta watched in amazement, it bit the other huge dog-beastie's head and ripped it right off!

The other dog-beasties, seeing this, realized they were way outmatched. They ran off in all directions. As Monsta watched in horrid fascination the giant chewed on the dog-beasties head and then swallowed it. Then it began biting pieces of its body.

Monsta carefully climbed out of the back of the bus, making sure the creature didn't see him. He was glad now he didn't try to talk to it, or he would have been its meal instead of the dog-beasties.

He crept back to his car and hopped inside. He sat and watched the giant creature finish its meal. And as he did, he came up with an even better plan. All he had to do was find a way to lure the monsters to New Sanctuary. There was no way Johnny's tribe could ever beat them. They would do what Ripper couldn't. Monsta pictured in his mind's eye what the creatures would do to the people of Johnny's tribe, and it warmed his evil heart. He would make sure Johnny and his tribe paid back the debt they owed with their deaths, and they would be very terrifying and grisly ones.

CHAPTER 6

Johnny and the adventurers poured onto the floor, relieved to be out of the darkness. Deecee trotted around, surveying the floor. It seemed to be empty, covered with dust and dirt. Rich red carpet, now turning brown from age, covered the floor. In front of them they could see rows and rows of tan colored cloth walls that ended four feet from the ground, connected to each other to make a maze of small spaces with desks filled with old 'lectric junk from before. Here and there, a path between the walls led to the wall beyond. At the wall windows going from the floor all the way to the ceiling showed the world outside.

Most of the windows were shattered, and a slight breeze blew in making a whistling sound through them. The few windows that were still intact were in the corners and covered with grime and dark. Light from the red eye lit up the room and made a large beam of light on the floor.

The air felt stale and dead, even with the wind blowing in, and there was a smell of mold in the air. Johnny and his friends reluctantly walked into the room, for it felt like a graveyard.

Deb saw something and recoiled in disgust. It was the body of a man from before sitting in a chair, his hands still poised over his 'lectric machine, just a skeleton covered with a few bits of skin and rotted clothes. To Deb, he looked like he could turn and talk to her at any moment, and she moved back to be closer to Johnny.

As they walked through the space, the dust in the carpet rose up in little puffs as the stepped on it, making them all feel sick. Deecee trotted around but couldn't find anything of interest, so he came back to walk next to Johnny.

"Wow, this place is creepy!" Super said. "No wonder you never came up here!"

Johnny led them towards the windows. "Let's just hope those black monsters lose interest pretty soon."

As they passed by the little spaces, they saw more corpses, some in chairs, others lying on the floor. One, a woman, hid under a desk, clutching a rotted, tattered black book that said, "B-I-B-L-E" on the cover.

Johnny and his friends reached the windows and,

careful not to be seen, looked down. There below them were hundreds of the black creatures! And in the front of them was the huge black leader, bigger than all the rest, with his gold chain and armbands.

"I don't think they're going to leave anytime soon, Johnny," Starbucks said, "I just hope they don't trash our Harleys."

"I don't think they will," Deb said. "They look too primitive to know what they are or care about them."

"What do you think they are, Johnny?" Super said, shuddering. "Were there creatures like that before?"

"I don't think so," Johnny replied. "I think they were caused by the mushroom monsters. Misterwizard talked about, 'meta-mophaseez that might cause mootashuns,' whatever that means."

Suddenly they heard a noise. They all turned with panic and looked towards the sound. There, they saw a man, standing watching them.

He was the oldest man Johnny had ever seen, and he was filthy and wearing dirty rags. He stood still on bony legs and stared at them; his eyes sad. He looked harmless and weak, and Johnny felt a pang of sympathy for him.

The man pointed a crooked finger at them, his eyes lighting up with a desperate hope. "People!" The man said in a trembling, old voice that cracked from lack of use.

Johnny looked at the others and they looked at him. They all agreed he looked harmless, so without a word they all approached him.

"Who are you?" Johnny asked.

The man wept and mumbled incoherently, and Johnny began to suspect mind was gone.

"Shhh! They'll hear!"

The man wept some more, turned and began shuffling away. Starbucks ran up and blocked his path. He put a gentle hand on him. "We're friends. Please tell us, what are they?" Starbucks pointed towards the windows where the monsters were.

"Black devils! One night they came up out of the sea. Ate everyone! Now we hide and starve. It's all we do.!"

He tried to walk around Starbucks, but Starbucks moved to block his path.

Suddenly from outside, they heard an ominous sound. Super ran over and looked out the window. She turned back with fright.

"They're climbing up the building!"

"You bring them here!" The old man screeched and ran around Starbucks. Starbucks went to chase him, but Johnny said, "Let him go, Starbucks. We have to find a way to escape ourselves!"

Lady Stabs knew she had to do something, or Johnny and his friends would be the horrible creatures' dinner. She stopped and thought, *What would Johnny do?* He'd try to create a distraction so the trapped people could escape, of course! But how? Lady Stabs looked around. She stood next to a tall building, but on the ground floor there were doors and windows showing all kinds of weird gadgets. One of the windows showed some fake people with women's clothes on them. Lady Stabs thought that it must have been where someone sold clothing before. But what could she possibly use it for? She thought hard, and then came up with a plan. It wasn't a great plan, but it was better than nothing.

A few minutes later, she stood on the second floor of the building near the windows. She stared down at the huge group of monsters. If her plan succeeded, the monsters would be coming after her instead of Johnny and his friends, and she knew she had to be ready to run, fast.

She was almost ready. She walked to the window carrying a big rock. Behind her stood twenty of the fake people, all lined up like an army. She breathed hard, steeled herself and then threw the rock with all her might!

It sailed out of the window in a long, graceful arc. Lady Stabs watched it, holding her breath. She looked up and smiled. Johnny, Deb and the others saw her! Johnny was smiling. Lady Stabs waved, embarrassed and a little ashamed. Johnny waved back, and then the other did too! They were glad to see her!

The rock landed, hitting one of the black creatures right on the head. It raised an arm to its head, screeched and turned to see who threw it. The monsters around it all turned to look too, and soon most of the monsters were looking in Lady Stabs' direction. Then they saw her!

Now was the time to go into her act. She had ropes tied to her wrists which she tied to some of the fake people. Moving her arms, she made the arms of the fake people move too. She hoped it would make the monsters think a whole army was attacking!

At first the monsters simply stared. Then the big black leader with is gold bracelets and necklace walked forward so it could see.

"Rowr row, rowr!" Lady Stabs snarled, trying to sound fierce. She had no illusions her little show would really scare them, she just hoped it distracted them long enough for Johnny and his friends to escape.

It seemed to be working! They all began walking

towards her building now. But with a sick feeling she realized the creatures weren't scared, they looked hungry! They thought the fake people were real and wanted to eat them!

Lady Stabs grinned. It was working! The first monsters reached her building and started climbing up the sides. Oh, oh, it was working! *Time to leave, Lady Stabs, and fast,* she thought.

She tried to run, but forgot to untie the ropes and was jerked back by the fake people, who fell on the floor. She fell on her back too and frantically tried to untie her wrists. She could hear the screeches of the monsters, and they were getting too close for comfort!

Monsta pushed on the pedal on the floor, waiting for the car to go. When nothing happened, he pushed the pedal again, then again, impatient, getting angry. Then he remembered something, laughed at himself and thought how dumb he was. You had to turn the metal thing you put in the slot next to the steering wheel first! He chuckled at himself, reached down, grabbed the metal thing sticking out of the from the dashboard and twisted it. A chugging sound came from the front, but nothing happened.

Oh, oh, Monsta thought. It couldn't be out of the strange water that made it go, could he? Not here, not now, of all times! No, he had poured a whole bunch in the little hole in the back where you put the water before he left Washington Deecee, and he knew it couldn't be all out yet. That meant there must be something else wrong.

Fear spread through Monsta's insides like an exploding mushroom monster. He didn't know a thing about fixing the cars, that was one of the gangers named Toolbin's job, back when there was a gang. He didn't even know what made them go. He just knew you turned the little metal thing, shifted the stick on the right, pushed a pedal on the floor and it moved, and you kept it from running into things by turning the wheel. Up to now, he didn't even know it could stop working. What was he going to do?

He looked over at the black monster. It was almost done eating the dog-beastie. When it was, it would surely look over and see him. He looked with fright down at the metal thing, grabbed it and turned it again. Once again, the chugging sound came. He pushed on the pedal again and again, willing it to go. Then he turned the metal thing again. The chugging came again, but it was fainter!

What was he going to do? Trapped in a city full of horrible black monsters who ate dog-beasties for lunch? What else did they eat? He glanced out the window in all directions and began to wish he'd never decided to come after Johnny. After all, Johnny had friends. Monsta was all alone.

And it's all Johnny's fault, he told himself. How he wanted to get revenge! But if he got eaten by a black monster, Johnny would win, and never even know Monsta was after him.

He reached down to try the metal thing again, and then in the corner of his eye he saw something. He looked out the window. Three more black monsters came running on their four legs towards him between two buildings on the right! He was going to be surrounded!

He whined, and wondered if he could just slink down and appear invisible, maybe they wouldn't even notice him. The thought of hiding like a cowardie made Monsta mad, but what choice did he have? The monsters were terrifying!

He slipped down so he wasn't visible from outside the car and watched the new monsters' approach. He began to realize they had slight differences. One was tall and thin; another was short and bulky. The third look smaller, as if it was a scrabbler monster. All three looked scary.

They passed by Monsta's car, and he secretly trembled, hoping they wouldn't notice him. His heart thumped loudly, so loud that he was afraid the monsters would hear it. His knees knocked and he clamped his legs together to stop them. He tried not to breathe.

The creatures walked up to the first one, who had just finished his dog-beastie. They screeched in some weird language Monsta couldn't understand. Listening to it, Monsta decided they were primitive creatures, maybe even some type of beastie.

Primitive or not, they could still rip Monsta apart. He decided to try to start the car one more time. He knew it might not start, just make a noise that would attract the monsters. If it did, he'd have to be ready to run, fast.

Looking down at the metal thing, he took a deep breath and turned it one more time.

CHAPTER 7

Johnny watched the black creatures climbing the building with dismay. Looking at them made his skin crawl, they reminded him of giant spider-beasties.

"Johnny," Deb yelled, "we're trapped!"

Then Super saw something and pointed straight ahead at something on the other side of the street. "Hey, look!"

They all looked where she pointed. Across the gray ribbon of street, over the heads of the monsters, they saw a figure in the next building. In fact, it looked like a whole group of people.

"Who's that?" Deb said, peering and trying to see that far.

"It looks like…" Super said.

"It is! What do you know?" Starbucks grinned.

"It's our old friend from home, Lady Stabs!"

Johnny looked perplexed. "What is she doing here?"

"She must have followed us," Deb said.

"And now she's trying to save our skins!" Super said with a grateful smile.

They all smiled, especially when they saw Lady Stabs pick up a big rock and hurl it far away from herself, out onto the crowd of monsters.

"What is she doing?" Starbucks asked.

"Trying to distract them," Johnny said. "She's putting herself in a lot of danger!"

Lady Stabs grinned and waved at them. They all waved back cheerfully.

The rock hit one of the monsters on the head and it howled. All the monsters climbing the building stopped, turned and looked over at the other building, along with ones on the ground.

Deecee growled, and Johnny quickly put a hand over his snout. "Shh, Deecee, now's not the time to get attention."

"Let's not waste time," Deb said. "Let's get back to our Harleys!"

"It looks like she has a whole crowd of people over there to help us!" Starbucks said.

"Look   closer,"   Johnny   said.   "They're   all

fake people."

"Oh yeah," Super said. "Clever!"

"Okay, back downstairs." Johnny held Deecee's collar and led the way back towards the door down. "And let's hope the monsters at the bottom take the bait, or we're going to be walking right into them."

They ran back towards the stairs, but suddenly Super tripped over the drawer of a desk lying on the ground. With a yell she fell on it.

"Super!" Starbucks yelled, running to her. The others ran towards her as well, worried.

Super lay on top of the drawer, her long, black hair draped over her face. Blood oozed from a cut on the front of her lower leg and she sat clutching it.

Starbucks put an arm around her and pulled her close. "Darling, are you okay?"

Super grinned sheepishly. "What a dummy!"

"No, you're not!" Deb said.

They all looked at Super's leg. Along with an inch long cut, it was turning blue with a big bruise.

Johnny glanced out the window, wondering where the monsters were. For the moment, they seem to be falling for Lady Stabs' trick. The ones on the building started back down again, and the horde in the street turned and moved towards the other building. Soon they saw the monsters begin to climb the other building.

"Poor Lady Stabs!" Deb said. "What if they catch her?"

"We have to worry about Super right now," Starbucks said. "Can you walk, Super?"

With Starbuck's help, Super stood up, keeping the injured leg off the ground.

"We have to find a way to bind her cut," Johnny said. "And get her out of here! Deb, see if you can find anything."

As Johnny and Starbucks supported Super on either side and helped her limp to the door, Deb searched the room for anything to use. She found an old scarf, faded and covered with dust.

"I found something, but it's not very clean." Deb shook it to try and get as much dust off as possible then hurried to join the others.

They stopped for a second and as Starbucks held Super, Johnny bound her leg with the scarf and tied it tight. Super's face looked drawn and white. Starbucks stared at her with alarm.

"We have to get her to Misterwizard!" Starbucks said.

"Right now, let's just get to safety, away from these monsters," Johnny replied.

Deb took another glance out the window. The monsters were fast. They had reached the second floor of the other building and from where they were, Johnny and the rest could see them grabbing the fake people, biting them, and realizing they'd been fooled, throwing them out the windows.

"I don't see Lady Stabs; she must have gotten away!" Starbucks yelled.

"Good!" Johnny said.

They made it to the door leading to the stairs. But then Deb turned and pointed. "Johnny, they're coming back!"

Johnny stopped, dismayed. "We're too late!"

Sure enough, the monsters, realizing they'd been fooled, came rushing back towards Johnny and his friends. The ones who had been climbing the building jumped on it again. It looked like, thanks to Super's injury, they were doomed once more.

Then they heard the loud rumble of an engine. All the monsters turned and looked towards the sound. Johnny and his friends ran back to the window to see what it was. What they saw was quite a sight.

Barreling down the road came a car driven by someone with long black hair who looked like a ganger, with a whole horde of monsters chasing him. With delight, the adventurers watched all the monsters drop off the building and the whole horde took off after the car. It seemed the monsters' attention span was not very long, and the closest and noisiest thing grabbed their attention.

"Yay! They're leaving!" Deb said. They all rushed back to the door. But just as they reached it, a huge, black monster stepped in their way. They were trapped!

Lady Stabs knew if she didn't get up in the next few seconds, her fate was sealed. She crawled backwards, dragging two of the fake people with her. The two she dragged bumped into other ones, making them move and seem alive.

The first creature jumped into the room! It shrieked in a thunderous voice and leapt on the closest fake people. Lady Stabs frantically fought at the ropes, and finally got one hand free. Another monster leapt into the room. It quickly bounded over and jumped on another fake people. Lady Stabs tried to lay perfectly still as she slowly worked on the rope tying her wrist, hoping they wouldn't notice her.

Another one leapt in, and then another! But now, the first one realized the trick and knew the fake people weren't real. It grabbed one of the fake people with two of its tentacled arms and threw it out the window. It sailed through the air like a child's toy to land far away down the street. The second one realized he'd been fooled as well and he leapt up and down on the fake people in anger. The two new monsters didn't bother to come in. They realized it was a trick and turned back to the windows. They screeched something at the ones climbing in the window, and soon they were all turning back. Lady Stab's trick hadn't worked that long, she just hoped it was long enough, and that it didn't cost her life.

She finally got her wrist free and began slowly, ever so slowly, inching her way towards the back steps. As she did, she looked out and saw the monsters were once again scaling Johnny's building. Did she buy them enough time?

Then she heard an engine roar outside. Forgetting her danger for a moment, she stood up and looked. She was in time to see Monsta roar down the street. As Lady Stabs watched with happiness, all the monsters climbed down and joined the mob chasing after him. Maybe they would all escape after all, thanks to the unlucky stranger in the car, whomever it was.

CHAPTER 8

The monster in front of Johnny and his friends was larger than most of the others, and his huge shape filled the room with a dark shadow. Its black, beady eyes burned with anger and something else: hunger. It held two long golden swords in its two lower arms, the ends of the arms wrapped around the handles and its suction cups helping to hold them. Its two upper arms waved around, as if it couldn't wait to have something to grab with them.

It leapt towards Johnny with a roar, so high it smashed into a chandelier hanging from the ceiling, causing it break free and fly across the room.

"Johnny, look out!" Deb yelled. Super stumbled away with Starbucks helping her.

Johnny dove at the last minute and the creature landed on the red carpet and caused a huge puff of dust to rise in the air like a ghost.

Johnny pulled out his own sword, which though sharp and curved, looked tiny compared to the ones the monster held. Starbucks took his sword out too and stood over Super, guarding her. Deb took out her knife, the one Johnny gave her, and she ran to stand at Johnny's side. Together they all faced the monster.

"Johnny, we don't have time for this!" Starbucks said.

"You take the girls and get out of here while I keep it occupied!" Johnny replied.

"No, we all leave here together, or not at all," Super said.

Starbucks let Super go and ran at the monster, who stomped towards him, its swords raised.

Suddenly Johnny ran past Starbucks, his sword held in both hands. Before the monster could react, Johnny slashed at its leg. Dark, black blood poured from the wound and the creature screeched and touched the wound with one of its upper arms.

Johnny didn't waste any time following up. He leapt in and stabbed the giant in the chest. It grabbed at the wound and slashed its swords in a deadly arc, but Johnny had already stepped out of the way.

Just then Deecee snarled and bit the giant on the ankle. It howled and tried to grab at Deecee, but Deecee pulled until the monster's leg came out from under it and it fell with loud thump.

As if not to be left out, Deb lunged forward and stabbed the giant right in its left eye. Blood poured from the eye and the creature screeched and slapped an arm over it. Even though it was much bigger than them, the monster seemed to realize it was outnumbered. It crawled backwards down the hallway.

Johnny and his friends cheered, raising their swords in victory. Deecee let go of the monster's leg and stood still, barking furiously at it. Johnny, Starbucks and Deb hugged and petted Deecee, who wagged his tail and panted happily.

"Let's not wait for it to come back!" Super said. She looked weak.

They all hurried to the door to the stairs, Starbucks supporting Super, eager to leave this little adventure behind.

Once again, they walked into the dark, musty stairway, this time going down. Deb dreaded the thought of going back into the dark pit again, and her stomach dropped. This time she clung to Johnny's arm. The others didn't seem to like it any better, for they all wore scared, unhappy expressions.

"Once more into the breech," Johnny said in the dark, his voice seeming to float on the air.

"What does that mean?" Super's voice sounded weak and frail in the dark.

"I don't know," Johnny said, his voice echoing of the stone walls.

"We know," Super said. "It's something Misterwizard said."

Despite the danger and Super's wound, they all laughed, happy to have something to release the tension, their voices mingling in the dark. Deb's spirits cheered a little. "The darkness is not so bad, now that I know what's there."

They reached the bottom and all of the rest waited for Johnny to see if it was safe. Johnny slowly opened the door. The hallway was empty! Their Harleys lay on their sides where the monsters had climbed over them. Johnny just hoped they weren't damaged.

"Hurry!" He whispered and ran out the door to his Harley. As the others piled out, Johnny picked up his Harley and started it up. It thundered comfortingly, and Johnny grinned. No matter how many times he'd ridden or what adventure he was in, the roar of his Harley still thrilled him when he started its engine.

Starbucks ran to his and lifted it off the ground. "Stupid monsters. No respect for people's property!" He turned the start button, grabbed the lever on the Harley's left handlebar and his Harley roared to life too.

"Hop in, Deecee!" Deecee dutifully climbed in his sidecar. Deb climbed on Johnny's Harley and Starbucks helped Super on his, careful to support her leg.

And just in time, for the monsters were not very far away, and at the sound of the engines, two ran back towards them. Johnny took off with Starbucks right behind. They sped down the hallway, looking for a way out. Soon the two monsters were right behind them! Johnny led them on a chase, around and around back into the large open area in the front and back down the hallway with the four double doors. The monsters screeched, their tentacled legs making loud thumping sounds on the floor.

Johnny spotted a broken window and pointed. "Out there!" He sped his bike towards it. It was behind a moldy old couch, and Johnny rode up the couch and out the window. Starbucks followed, with Super yelling, "Yipes!" as they sailed out into space.

Lady Stabs hurried to her Harley and jumped on, happiness spreading through her like heat from the red eye. She'd helped Johnny and his friends escape, and it looked like she was going to get away too! She started her Harley and sped off towards the nearest street, where a soft breeze blew paper in the air past old rusted cars and skeletons. Even though it looked lonely and desolate, to Lady Stabs it reminded her of an imaginary place she remembered being told about once called Heaven after what she'd just been through.

She still didn't know where Johnny and Starbucks were, she realized, and so was no better off than before. She decided despite the danger, she needed to circle back around the other building and see if her friends were still in trouble. She realized she may have to give her life to save them, and she was okay with that. Johnny has saved her from a life with the Gangers, and for that she owed him her life already.

She drove slowly, keeping her eyes out for more black monsters, but it seemed whomever was in that car had drawn all of the creatures' attention. The streets were safe, but she knew only for a few moments.

She reached the intersection where she could see the other building to her left. It looked empty now, dead, even peaceful, not a person or creature in sight. Looking at it, no one would have known seconds ago it had been the scene of a strange and bizarre, terrifying struggle.

She drove down the street next to the building, listening for any sound, looking for any sight of her friends. She decided she'd do a circle all the way around it and look for them. She stopped for a moment and listened, to see if she could catch any sound of them. Then he heard a strong, masculine voice. She smiled, think it must be Johnny and his friends.

She turned around and looked, and her smile instantly disappeared to be replaced by a look of fear and dismay. Someone had caught her, and it didn't look like a friend.

CHAPTER 9

Monsta drove as fast as he could, his mind blank with fear. What had he gotten himself into? He spun the steering wheel crazily, trying to weave around junk cars and old buses. Here and there, old rusted metal containers that had once been called mailboxes, now just rusted hunks of steel also dotted the road. All the time, fear gripped his insides, fear that the road ahead would be blocked and the creatures would catch him.

He glanced behind and wished he hadn't. There were hundreds of them! They filled the street and the sidewalks, from the front of the building on the left all the way to the one on the right. They were all big and fierce, some with colored armbands or different colored streamers attached to their arms. They all screeched, intent on catching him and killing him for their dinner.

Ahead, Monsta saw a large opening. As he grew closer to the border of the city, there were less buses and subway cars. Ahead, the open road beckoned. He was going to make it!

Just then the car lurched and wheezed. Oh, no, it was dying! Not now!

Sure enough, the car slowed down. He pushed hard on the pedal on the floor that was supposed to make it go. The car made a roaring sound each time he did, but didn't move much faster. Could he be out of the special water that made it go? Could the strange contraption under the hood be broken?

He looked back again, and as saw with fright that the monsters were gaining on him. Why didn't they give up?

He saw something ahead that gave him some hope. It was a herd of deer-beasties munching on a small patch of grass that had grown up in a courtyard of a building. Hope sprang up in him that the animals would distract the black monsters.

Sure enough, as he passed by the deer-beasties, the whole crowd of monsters turned and took off after them. The deer-beasties sprang away with the monsters in pursuit.

Monsta laughed. What a bunch of silly, dumb creatures the monsters were, not more than beasties themselves, easily distracted by anything. Still, he wasn't out of danger yet. If his car died, what would he do?

Suddenly as if reading his thoughts, the car ground to a halt, hissed and went silent. Monsta cursed it and beat on the steering wheel, furious.

He climbed out of the car and gazed at the buildings and street behind him. Were any of the creatures still following him?

He didn't see any of them, and the only sound was the whistling of the wind. The city looked deserted again, the old buildings on either side of the street dirty and broken, like two old men asleep. Rusted old cars lined the street, one on the sidewalk halfway inside the window of a building. The remnants of skeletons lie in the street, looking like they were merely sleeping.

Monsta sighed with relief and tried to decide what to do. Should he try and fix his car, or leave while he had the chance? Either way, he'd lost his prey, Johnny and his friends. He doubted he'd ever find them again. The thought disappointed and angered him. What magical power did Johnny have that he always seemed to escape from danger?

He kicked the car door savagely, leaving a new dent to join all the others. He decided he'd take one look at the contraption in the front, though he didn't have a clue how to fix it. He opened the hood and peered down at the engine, which smoked, steamed and hissed. He didn't have a clue what to look at, so he just stared at it dumbly. It all looked good to him. He decided he'd see if anything looked broken or loose.

He touched the top of the engine, howled and immediately jumped back. It was hot! He put his burnt finger in his mouth, sucked on it and stepped back. This was going to be tougher than he imagined.

Then he saw movement, something black, out of the corner of his eye.

He looked back at the city. Sure enough, two of the black monsters ran towards him, their eyes fixed on him with dark intent. He cursed his luck It seemed as if not all the monsters followed the deer-beasties, at least two were looking for other prey.

The monsters held long clubs with spikes. One had missing arm from an earlier battle. The other was one of the shortest Monsta had seen, but he was thick and tough looking. Monsta bet he would be the tougher of the two to fight.

Monsta had no intention of fighting either of them. He grabbed his weapon bag out of the car, turned and ran. He cast one more look at the car, missing it already. Now he would be on foot in a strange land, miles from any place he knew. And he was already being pursued by two monsters. He thought he might be able to take one of the creatures but not two. As the red eye beat down on him, he hurried towards the end of the buildings and the rows of smaller houses beyond.

Then he saw something strange. A woman sat on a Harley, just like Johnny's, but it wasn't Johnny or his friends. Monsta hurried towards the person, trying to keep quiet. Whoever they were, they would provide him with another means of transportation, whether they liked it or not.

Monsta walked up to Lady Stabs, a dark look of menace on his face. As he grew closer, Lady Stabs recognized who he was. She remembered him from the gang. He was not very bright, but he was big, and mean, and not someone to tangle with. Many gangers had ended up with broken arms or missing teeth for crossing him or being foolish enough to fight him. Lady Stabs thought back and then remembered what they called him: Monsta.

He walked slowly towards her, and she saw he recognized her too by the look in his eyes. Fear fluttered in her stomach, for she knew he could easily kill her if he wanted to. Did he know that she had aligned herself with

Johnny and his tribe? She wasn't sure.

"I know you," Monsta said, pointing a big, meaty finger at her. Then he smiled, and Lady Stabs realized instantly the look of desire in his eyes. "You're Lady Stabs."

She smiled at him warmly, invitingly. "And you're Monsta, the big, handsome ganger, and Ripper's second in command."

Lady Stabs knew Monsta would like the compliment, and sure enough Monsta grinned bigger. But then he frowned with puzzlement. "What are you doing here?"

Lady Stabs thought fast. "The same thing as you, heading back to our old home to try and remake the Doomsday Prophecy."

Monsta snorted with disgust, and he waved a big hand. "Without Ripper?"

Lady Stabs glanced behind Monsta, and her heart leapt with hope. In the far distance, she saw two Harleys approaching. It had to be Johnny and Starbucks! If she could just stall Monsta until they arrived, together they could beat him. She smiled and tried to act happy.

"Why not? There are two of us. I bet there are more, still around. But we'd need a new leader."

Monsta stood up a little taller and his eyes lit up, understanding she meant him. But then he scowled dark and deep.

"First, we must kill Johnny for what he did to Ripper and our gang. We must rip his arms out of their sockets and tear his heart out!"

Monsta demonstrated each action in pantomime. "But first we will kill his friends in front of him and do lots of nasty things to his girlfriend."

Monsta reminded Lady Stabs of Ripper, and her insides twisted. She frowned with disgust. Monsta smiled with evil pleasure at the thought of what he was planning to do. He turned and looked at Lady Stabs with suspicion.

"Don't you want to see Johnny pay?"

Lady Stabs put on a fake smile and nodded vigorously. "Of course. His whole tribe has to pay, but first we need to grow strong again, get the gang back together…"

"No!" Monsta took a threatening step towards Lady Stabs and she backed up in fear. "We kill Johnny first! That's what Ripper would want!"

Monsta strode up until he was only inches away from Lady Stabs, a murderous look on his face, his hands balled into fists. "Where were you, during the fight?"

Lady Stabs looked past Monsta again. Johnny and his friends were only a block away, if she could just stall him…

"I was fighting like everybody else!"

"Then you will help me kill Johnny." Monsta waited for a reply, watching her very closely

"Of course, I will!"

"Good. My car broke. We will ride together."

Monsta jumped on the Harley and motioned with his hand for her to follow. "We need to find them again. Then we will get our revenge."

Lady Stabs saw Johnny and his friends out of the corner of her eye. They rode behind them from the city only a block away, coming towards them. Lady Stabs tried to distract Monsta until Johnny could get there and help her. "I think you liked me, didn't you, Monsta?"

Monsta grinned and smiled at her with obvious desire, and Lady Stabs grinned for real, sure her trick had worked.

"Hurry and get on!" Monsta barked. "I think they are already ahead of us!"

Monsta motioned for her to climb on. Just then, the sound of Johnny's Harley roaring echoed in the air. Monsta turned around and looked. When he saw Johnny and his friends his eyes went wide. "Get on now, before they see us!"

Lady Stabs had no choice but to comply. She climbed on the Harley, panic and dismay filling her. Why couldn't Johnny and Starbucks ride just a little faster?

As she glanced backwards and watched with sadness, Monsta started the Harley and took off. She kept gazing at Johnny and Starbucks until they disappeared behind them when they rode over a hill. She was really trapped now, with a dangerous madman, and if she wasn't careful, the first person he killed would be her.

Back on the road, Johnny and his friends took off as fast as they could. Behind them, the city seemed eerily quiet, but their nerves were tense, wondering if more monsters would appear.

Deb looked over her shoulder and her eyes widened with renewed fear. There behind them four blocks away the spider-like creatures massed. As far as she could tell, they hadn't seen them, but it would only be a matter of seconds before they did. "Johnny, they're behind us, but pretty far back," she said.

Starbucks turned his head, trying to look at Super. He felt her head laying on his back, but she didn't seem to be moving. He was getting really scared.

"Johnny, what are we going to do about Super?"

"Let's get her to Pill-a-delpia. We can take her to

Misterwizard's castle there. I bet he has lots of things to fix her up."

Starbucks smiled worriedly, but with hope. Johnny always seemed to have a plan.

Johnny gave the Harley more power and sped forward faster.

"Hey, Johnny, look!" Starbucks pointed ahead of them as he stared at what he saw in the distance.

Johnny looked too. There three blocks away in the middle of the road stood two people talking next to a Harley a lot of Johnny and Starbuck's. In the foreground they saw the car that earlier sped off, chased by the monsters. It sat smoking and looked abandoned.

"Johnny, It's Lady Stabs!" Super yelled over the sound of the Harleys. "But who's that with her?"

Deecee watched the figures ahead too and barked. Then he looked at the man next to Lady Stabs and growled.

"I don't know!" Johnny yelled. Johnny made the Harley go as fast it he could. Starbucks saw what Johnny did and speeded up too.

As they grew close, they saw the other figure was a man, a big man, in Ganger clothes. Johnny and his friends didn't recognize him, though Johnny though he looked familiar.

Then just before they could get to them, the man

climbed on the Harley. Lady Stabs joined him, and they sped away.

"She's leaving with him, Johnny!" Deb yelled. "Who is he?"

Before Johnny and his friends could get near, the other Harley drove away, too fast for them to catch it. Johnny stopped so Starbucks did too. He sat on his Harley and watched the other bike disappear over the horizon.

"Why did you stop, Johnny?"

Johnny pondered what they'd just seen, and then after a pause answered.

"Lady Stabs just saved us. Now she's leaving with that man. I didn't recognize him, but he looked like one of the Gangers. I swear I saw him during the battle for Sanctuary."

"Do you think he's kidnapping her?" Super asked.

"But she seemed to get on the Harley like she wanted to," Deb added.

"That doesn't mean she had a choice, though," Starbucks said.

Johnny looked ahead. They were almost at the northern edge of the city. Ahead of them, Pill-a-delpia beckoned.

"Let's keep going but keep our eyes peeled. We need to go a little quieter now. If that man has Lady

Stabs as a prisoner, chances are he's doing it to get to us. We have to make sure we see him before he sees us."

"How do we peel our eyes?" Deb asked.

"But Johnny," Starbucks said with a dark look. "What if, and I know this is not a nice thing to think, but what if she decided to rejoin the Gangers?"

"She wouldn't do that," Deb said crossly. Then she glanced at Johnny with a look of uncertainty. "Would she, Johnny?"

"Of course not. She just tried to save us. But we have no way of knowing who that man was, or why she's going with him. We're just going to have to be careful until we find out."

"But Johnny, we have to get Super to Misterwizard's!" Deb said.

Johnny nodded silently. They were torn between two choices. "I know. We're going to have to take care of Super first. Then just hope we can find Lady Stabs, and make sure she's all right."

Johnny started his Harley again, a look of regret on his face, and slowly motored forward. Starbucks followed; sorry their predicament might cost Lady Stabs her life.

CHAPTER 10

The black monsters watched the strange visitors speed away. The tall black leader strode up and they parted for him and turned to listen to what he said. It screeched in a loud, angry voice, and they all screeched back in return.

They all shook their swords in the air with fury. Then slowly one by one turned and headed back towards the city. The black leader stood watching the horizon long after Johnny and his friends were gone. Then slowly it too turned and walked away.

But unseen by anyone, one monster continued down the street, following Johnny and his friends.

Johnny and Starbucks sped along down the winding, gray road of rock, past old cars and buses. In the distance more cities could be seen, smaller, some looking like just visions shimmering in the noon-day heat. Johnny vowed he would visit all of them, some day.

"Man, am I glad to leave that place behind, and in one piece!" Starbucks yelled.

"Amen!" Super said, not raising her head, repeating a word she'd heard said in similar circumstances, though she didn't know what it meant.

Soon Ball-tim-moree was left far behind. They passed house and empty fields, and for a moment relaxed. The dangers they had just been through faded like a bad dream, and soon they were smiling and enjoying themselves again.

They reached Pill-a-delpa, the twisted buildings black against the orange sky. They all gazed on the city, remembering their adventures here.

"Wow," Deb said. "I never thought I'd see this place again."

"I wonder if any of the Doomsday Prophecy are still hanging around." Starbucks said. "We need to hurry to Misterwizard's place Johnny, for Super's sake."

"Yes, we will," Johnny replied.

A pang of home sickness hit Johnny, stronger than he expected, and he thought how he couldn't wait to see Misterwizard's old castle. He even wanted to go back to old Sanctuary and see it again, even though he'd always hated it.

The rest just gazed at the city, quiet, as if lost in

some memory of their own. Johnny didn't stop, but just kept motoring along, into the city, past old buildings and cars. They drifted to the west, close to the river Johnny had crossed so long ago when he started his adventures. Then they started motoring down random streets, looking up at the tall buildings around them, empty squares shooting up into the sky, windowless and lonely.

Then Johnny did slow down, and Starbucks saw and did too.

"There!" Johnny pointed to a tall gray skyscraper with concrete steps leading up to a set of mostly smashed glass doors. Letters on the side of the building said Sh ps t Lib rt Plac."

There were not enough of them for even Johnny to understand what it said. "That's where the place was where we found our swords, remember Starbucks?"

"Do you think there's any of them left?" Super asked.

"No," Johnny said. "I gave them all to the Tribe, for our trip to Washington Deecee."

"Then why are we stopping?" Starbucks asked.

Johnny shrugged and drove on. Starbucks looked at Super and they grinned, sharing an understanding. Johnny was reliving his adventures. Starbucks sped up to catch up to Johnny.

They began to drift more east, towards the huge

water on their right that spanned the whole length of the city. It had been too far away for Johnny to reach on his adventures, for Sanctuary was far to the west and across the river from where they were now, and Johnny looked at it with interest. They were motoring through a part of the city Johnny had never been to before now, and he enjoyed seeing new buildings and streets to explore.

Suddenly they came upon a huge wall spanning the street made of metal, wood and trash. It was just like the walls Johnny's tribe had built in Washington Deecee. The wall ran right to the water's edge on the right and as far as they could see on the left. Some of the building blocks for this wall were old rusted cars and buses, just like the wall the Tribe built. In the middle of the wall stood a large gate made of wood slats and metal bars tied together. The wall was ten feet high and looked impregnable.

"Now what?" Starbucks said in a weary voice.

Johnny stopped at the wall, and they all gazed at it. "This definitely wasn't here before," Johnny said. "Could the Doomsday Prophecy have made it?"

Super raised her head weakly and stared at the wall, intrigued even though she was so tired. "They don't have the brains."

A tall, thin, old black man with white hair appeared at the top of the wall! He had on a green vest that went all the way to his knees with a white silhouette of the head of some angry bird on the front. He held a longbow in his hands with an arrow already cocked and ready to fire.

"Halt! Who approaches Pelpia?"

The adventurers looked at each other, then back at the man.

Johnny responded, trying to sound friendly and not threatening. "We used to live here. This was our city, Pill-a-delpia. Can you tell me who you are, and why you've put up these walls?"

Two more men appeared, both wearing the same vests, one short but stocky with a body like a block of wood carrying a sword and the other young, in his twenty seasons of medium height but strong with a lance.

"I know not what you speak, oh intruder. This is Pelpia, ruled by Mayr Restaria. We are the Letfreedomring, and we have owned this city forever!"

"He's not telling the truth, Johnny," Deb said. "We've only been gone for one season."

"But we never really came this way before," Johnny replied, rubbing his chin, thinking. "It's possible they started it while the Doomsday Prophecy was still here."

"Do you know who this is?" Starbucks said in a

lofty tone. "This is the great Johnny Apocalypse, and this is his city!"

Starbucks didn't expect his words to make much of an impact, but he was completely mistaken. The three men's faces filled with surprise and awe, but the black man with the longbow recovered quickly and looked suspicious again, not convinced.

"You truly be the great Johnny Apocalypse? We have heard tales of the man, his exploits, how it was he who destroyed the evil gangers and drove them from the land. If you truly are him and come in peace, we will welcome you. But how do we know you speak the truth?"

The second short stocky man with brown hair said to the first in a low voice, "It is him! Look, he rides the legendary chariot we've heard speak of!"

Johnny and his friends looked at each other and grinned, surprised but happy to see that they were becoming famous.

"Yes, I am the great Johnny Apocalypse," Johnny said, putting on airs to impress them like Misterwizard did, "And I deign to speak with Mayr Restaria of important matters."

Starbucks, Super and Deb laughed. Deb slugged Johnny in the side, trying to chastise him. Johnny took the hint and stopped goofing around. He started talking normal again.

"Listen, we come as friends. I am Johnny, and these are my friends Starbucks, Super and Deb. Our member Super is hurt, and she needs attention right away. Please help us."

The men whispered to each other in hushed tones of excitement. The tall, thin black man spoke and the others listened.

"Don't tell me we're going to have another fight on our hands," Deb said wearily. "I don't know if I have it in me. I'm ready for a nap."

The tall, thin black man, who seemed to be in charge, turned and spoke. "Johnny Apocalypse and friends, we believe you are who you say for now. We have heard you are a good man who fights evil, and so you are welcome in Pelpia. I am Johnthebaptist and will do anything to help you. But," Johnthebaptist said with a serious tone, "if you are fooling us, beware. We kill spies and enemies."

The two other men left and in a moment the gate creaked open loudly. Johnny and his friends smiled at each other, feeling relieved, but wondering what new adventure they were about to face.

Super squeezed Starbuck's middle and laid her head on his back. "Just give us a nice, warm bed and some of Misterwizard's spagetta."

They all laughed as Johnny and Starbucks rode past the gate. They stopped next to Johnthebaptist.

"Follow me." Johnthebaptist walked slowly, and Johnny and Starbucks puttered along next to him. A crowd began to form and follow, men, women and scrabblers all pointing at them with interest and whispering amongst themselves.

Behind them unseen, the black monster who had followed them watched, and then silently turned and left, back the way it had come.

Lady Stabs held onto Monsta's back as he drove the Harley further and further away from Ball-ti-imoree. He was not much of a talker, just stared ahead, and she remembered more about him now. He wasn't very bright, but he grew angry very easily, and he was intensely loyal to Ripper. She remembered how when one man had argued with Ripper a long time ago when they were back in Pill-a-delpia, Monsta had grabbed the man's hand and crushed it. Monsta would be very angry that Ripper was dead, and very dedicated to getting revenge. Lady Stabs knew he was even more dangerous now then he was before.

To her surprise Monsta stopped the Harley, turned his head and looked back at her and spoke, making her jump and her heart skip a beat. Looking at his dark, dead eyes and scars made her feel queasy.

"We need to plan now. Where is Johnny going you think?"

Lady Stabs didn't answer, not sure what to say.

Monsta turned around and stared forward. "To Misterwizard's, I bet. We should go there and hide."

Lady Stabs tried to think quickly. This was her chance to lead him away from Johnny, if she could. Lady Stabs had no doubt that's exactly where Johnny and his friends were heading, but she had to come up with a reason for Monsta to doubt it. She thought hard, her mind racing. "No! I heard them talking. They said they were headed to a city called New Ork, beyond Pill-a-delpia."

Monsta looked angry, sensing a trap. "Why would they go there? Why not go home to Sanctuary?"

"Misterwizard told them to go there, to make allies." *Good thinking,* she thought. *But will he buy it?*

Monsta turned to look at her again, and fear bubbled inside her. What if he suddenly suspected her? He could easily kill her, and no one would ever even know about it. She had no one to help her. She was all alone in the wasteland, just her and this monster.

She waited for what seemed like an eternity as he just stared forward. It looked like he was thinking, and Lady Stabs thought to herself that not being very bright, it wasn't easy for him. She chuckled inside at her humor, despite the danger.

Finally, he spoke. "So, he thinks to unite with other tribes and grow stronger, just like he did before. Soon he will be too big to fight. We must hurry and get there first. We will spread a web of lies. Then we will see what kind of welcome Johnny gets."

Monsta took off again in a roar. Lady Stabs sighed with relief. He'd bought her ruse! But then she thought of what that meant. It meant she was heading to a new city, a strange place they'd never been before. Who knew what evil men or monsters lived there? And she was going there with a man who would kill her without even the slightest hesitance, if he found out where her true loyalty lay.

As they continued on, Lady Stabs felt an intense sense of loneliness, and despair. Would she survive her captivity? Would she ever see Johnny, Misterwizard or any of the people of the Tribe again? She had no way of knowing.

CHAPTER II

Johnny and his friends motored along slowly next to Johnthebaptist, surrounded by the crowd. Johnny looked at the symbol on the Johnthebaptist's vest and realized most of the men in the army wore it as well. It was a regal white bird-beastie on a green background.

"This symbol, what is it?" Johnny asked "I remember seeing it in Phil-a-, I mean Pelpia before when we lived here."

Johnthebaptist smiled with pride. "This is the symbol of Letfreedomring. It is the great eagle. It has always been the symbol of Pelpia."

Johnny thought back and remembered how he had seen that symbol many times in the stores of Sanctuary. He had even seen carved wooden statues of the bird-beastie, almost as if it was an idol, and the symbol on strange round helmets with white bars on the front and green shirts with numbers on the back. He had never really known what it meant, or attached any significance to it before.

Deb marveled at what she saw around her. "Johnny, look how organized they look! All the trash is gone and they're living in the buildings again."

"They don't look like wildies, either," Starbucks said. "They look clean and well fed."

"I can't believe it!" Super said. "Look what they accomplished, in just the little time since we left!"

"Once the Doomsday Prophecy were gone, it looks like they were finally able to start creating a decent society," Johnny said.

"They look more organized than us!" Starbucks said. "We really need to tell Misterwizard about all this!"

Johnny nodded. There was so much already to share with Misterwizard, and yet they couldn't go back now, not until they found out what had happened to Lady Stabs.

Suddenly there was a murmuring amongst the crowd, and they all stopped. Johnny and Starbucks stopped their Harleys, for the crowd blocked their way. They looked at each other and at the crowd, wondering what was going to happen now.

Johnthebaptist stopped next to them, looking curious himself.

The crowd parted and two men stepped up, holding hands. As soon as the adventurers saw them, their mouths opened wide in surprise and shock. Starbucks pointed at them. "Look, Johnny, who it is!"

Johnny nodded. "It's Jewelrydept and Bargainbin."

Jewelrydept was a large muscular man with wavy black hair wearing a rough cotton shirt with no sleeves and a pair of black pants. Bargainbin was slender, with long brown hair that fell to his shoulders. He wore a white blouse and a black dress that went down to his ankles.

"Yes, it's Jewelrydept and Bargainbin," Jewelrydept said, his voice spitting bitterness. "You thought we died, didn't you? You sent us out into the Forbidden Wasteland, to die of the Sickness, all because of our love for each other."

Johnny, Starbucks, Deb and Super just stared for a moment, feeling ashamed and embarrassed. Then Starbucks shook his head. "You know it wasn't our fault you had to leave the Tribe, Jewelrydept. It was Leader Nordstrom."

Bargainbin's eyes blazed with fury and he pointed a finger at them like a knife. "Leader Nordstrom started it, but you stood by and watched!"

Johnny felt shame but anger too, for he and his

friends had nothing to do with it. He did remember the day Jewelrydept and Bargainbin were forced to leave. As everyone hid behind a glass door in one of the rooms, a door at the end of the Main Hall was opened by two enforcers holding ropes from as far away as they could stand. Johnny could still remember the light of the red eye streaming in and making a spear of light on the floor. Then Jewelrydept and Bargainbin, who stood next to the door, took one more look at the Tribe hiding behind the glass wall, took each other's hand and walked out. The door was shut then with a long wooden stick. Then the enforcers secured it again with wood and old nails.

Johnny was only ten seasons when it happened, and he was still scared of the outside then. Everyone was sure Leader Nordstrom was sending them to their doom, because they were both men who wanted to be mates. Johnny didn't understand everything that was happening, but even then, he had a feeling that what was happening to them wasn't fair. Later, Johnny's father Foodcourt and his mother Teavanna talked about it at dinner, how terrible it was and how the men would surely die in a matter of days.

"We were only scrabblers, Jewelrydept," Starbucks said. "We couldn't do anything."

Jewelrydept snorted. "Your parents could have. They could have stood up to Leader Nordstrom. But all they did was hide behind that wall and watch.”

Deb looked sorrowful and sad. “I'm sorry, Jewelrydept, Bargainbin. Nobody wanted to make you go. I think people were just too afraid of Leader Nordstrom.”

“And don't you remember,” Starbucks said. “Leader Nordstrom almost kicked me and my family out too, because of our color.” Starbucks turned and gazed at Super, who smiled back at him with humor and affection. “It was only because of Super's family that I got to stay. They fought Leader Nordstrom and got all the other families to argue until he gave up.”

Super walked close to Starbucks and they held hands. “And that's when I met you,” she said.

Starbucks grinned, his heart full of love and affection. “And that was the best day of my life.”

They leaned forward and touched foreheads, smiling at each other. Johnny and Deb smiled too watching them. Even Jewelrydept and Bargainbin were touched, and they watched them, then turned and gazed at each other with affection.

“It doesn't matter now. Leader Nordstrom is gone,” Johnny said. “The Tribe is led by Misterwizard and my father Foodcourt now, and things are different. I know the Tribe would accept you now.”

Jewelrydept frowned darkly again and he and

Bargainbin stared at Johnny and his friends again.

"We don't need your tribe anymore, Johnny. The people of Letfreedomring accept us for what we are. They believe in freedom and liberty for all."

"So do we!" Johnny said. "Misterwizard is trying to restore Mocracy."

"So, you say," Bargainbin said.

Johnthebaptist stepped forward and everyone looked at him. He turned to Jewelrydept and Bargainbin. "Jewelrydept, you seem to know these people. He claims to the be the great Johnny Apocalypse who destroyed the Doomsday Prophecy. Are they who they claim, or are you saying we should throw them out?"

Everyone looked at Jewelrydept and Bargainbin, including the crowd surrounding them. Everyone waited silently to see what the men would say.

Jewelrydept and Bargainbin looked at each other. Then they leaned towards each other and whispered. Jewelrydept nodded. He turned to Johnthebaptist.

"We too have heard of the great Johnny Apocalypse. And we knew Johnny and his friends when they were just scrabblers." He paused and looked at Johnny and Bargainbin smiled. "What he and his friends say is true. Their families were always good to us, even after everyone found out about us. We will not hold a grudge against them. As far as we are concerned, they should be welcomed."

The crowd cheered, and Johnny and his friends sighed with relief and smiled. Johnthebaptist smiled too. He turned to Johnny.

"You have just passed another test that proves you are who you claim. I think we can now truly welcome you into Pelpia, Johnny and friends. Please, let me take you to our Mayr, Restaria. She will want to meet you."

"Lead on, McDuff," Super said, something she heard Misterwizard say. The others looked at her and laughed. They all climbed back on the Harleys and followed Johnthebaptist again.

"Can you please tell us where you are taking us?" Johnny asked Johnthebaptist, who seemed to be in no hurry, taking each step deliberately, almost as if they were in some kind of formal procession. They had turned down many side streets, both left and right, and Johnny began to feel hopelessly lost.

"To the captol, also known as the Bell House, the place where Restaria our mayr resides."

The adventurers all looked at each other and shrugged, sharing the same curiosity.

"What's a mayr?" Deb asked Johnny.

Johnny answered, "I don't know."

"Just don't tell me it's a new kind of monster," Deb said. "I'm so tired, I'd just tell it to go ahead and eat me."

Johnny chuckled and realized he felt the same way. They were all exhausted.

Soon they approached a tall square building made of bricks with three rows of windows on the front. A tall white square tower rose in the middle of roof. On the front of the tower was a circle with two sticks on it, pointing in different directions.

Long green banners were draped over the sides of the building with the symbol of Pelpia on them. At the top of the square tower another round dome stood even higher, with long vertical windows. The windows were open, and through them they could see a strange brown colored object that looked like an upside-down flower hanging. At the very top of the brown dome, a tall white spike shot up into the air. It was a very impressive looking building and Johnny and his friends gazed at it with interest and fascination.

Suddenly Johnny and his friends jumped, for a loud, shrill sound rang from the top of the building. They saw the mushroom object moving back and forth, and each time it did the sound came again. It rang again, and again. It wasn't an unpleasant sound, but it was so loud that it seemed to penetrate into their bones and hurt their ears.

The people all around them began to chatter excitedly. It seemed as if their presence was being announced. As Johnny and his friends watched, more people came running from all directions.

Starbucks pointed towards the top of the building. "It's from that metal thing up there! That must be the bell!"

Johnny and his friends smiled at each other, excited that they were seeing and experiencing so many new things on their adventure. They were asked to get off their Harleys and were escorted inside the tall, stately square building. Starbucks helped Super to walk, and Deecee padded along beside Johnny panting good-naturedly.

As they entered the hall, Johnny realized it reminded him a lot of New Sanctuary, with fabric covered walls full of paintings, a marble floor and benches and elegant looking couches. In front of them, a sweeping marble staircase led to the upper level.

They were led to the middle of the floor. There they were made to wait. All the people looked expectantly up towards the staircase, and Johnny and his friends did too, wondering what was going to happen next.

As they watched with interest, a tall, elegant woman who looked to be about forty-five seasons or so in a long, dark blue cloak holding a long, gnarled cane appeared at the top of the staircase and started to walk down in an elegant and stately manner.

Her long, brown hair cascaded down on either side of her face, which was long and narrow, with a large sloping nose, and dark brown eyes that made her look mysterious, and yet she had a kind, gentle face. She instantly reminded Johnny of Misterwizard, and somehow, he seemed to know almost with certainty that she was a good person, just like his old friend.

She looked like what Johnny thought a real wizard should look like, and he wondered for a moment if she was one, but then dismissed the idea as silly. Still, he had a real feeling that Misterwizard and her would get along splendidly. She showed no fear, just eyes full of that concern that Johnny recognized as the look of a leader for her people. She walked right up to Johnny and his friends and stopped. She didn't appear threatening, just cautious. She smiled warmly but with some guardedness at them.

"Visitors on your strange machines and wearing the clothing of the Doomsday Prophets. And yet I am told, you are none other than the great Johnny

Apocalypse, whose courage and strength ridded this land of the Doomsday Prophecy, allowing me to organize our people and rebuild our society.

"I am Restaria, the mayr of Pelpia. If you truly are who you say you are, you will be welcomed with open arms. But if you lie, we will find out, and respond accordingly."

Johnthebaptist stepped forward with eyes full of excitement.

"He is the great Johnny Apocalypse! Jewelrydept and Bargainbin knew him! And he rides the silver chariot!"

A murmur went through the crowd, and Johnny saw Restaria react, though she was very careful not to show it. He could see a new respect for them in her eyes, and she smiled with curiosity.

Johnny couldn't help but swell with pride, though he pushed the feeling away. Now was not the time for him to get a swelled head and forget himself; they might be in a lot of danger.

Restaria turned back to Johnny. "And do you, Johnny Apocalypse, have some way to prove you are who you say you are? We have had many men, even amongst our own, claim to be the great Johnny Apocalypse, mostly when they've had too much of the strange water or are trying to impress their lady friends.

But a few came from other lands and were only trying to spy on us or find a weakness. We dealt with them most severely."

Johnny and his friends looked at each other, wondering what to say. Then Deb piped up. "He's Johnny, all right. We just came from Washington Deecee, where we fought the Doomsday Prophecy and defeated them. We have come back to visit the home of our old friend Misterwizard."

At the mention of Misterwizard, a new round of oohing and aahing came from the crowd.

"What do you want us to do to prove it to you?" Starbucks said.

Johnthebaptist piped up. "Where did you live when you were here?"

"At Sanctuary, on the other side of the river," Deb said.

More murmuring and nods.

"Look, this is all fun, but I hurt my leg. So can we get all this stuff over with?" Super said grumpily.

"And we have a friend who we think has been kidnapped," Johnny added. "She's riding with a man on a Harley much like ours. We need to find her before something bad happens to her."

Restaria smiled. "I believe you truly are the great Johnny Apocalypse this time. You and your friends are welcome in our kingdom."

The people all cheered, and Johnny and his friends all relaxed and smiled, glad the test was over.

"Come," Restaria said, motioning with her hand. "We will help heal your wounded member. Our Medicine Man Arrex has many healing balms and magical potions."

Restaria turned and walked towards the entrance. Johnny and his friends turned and followed, and the crowd tagged along around them, watching with happy interest.

On one wall a large hand-drawn map had been hung, showing different cities and paths running between them. Johnny walked over to the map and studied it.

"Restaria, what does this map mean?"

Restaria walked over to stand next to Johnny. She pointed at the map.

"This is a map of Marica," she said, "as much as we have yet explored or had told to us."

"Is that what you call our land?" Johnny asked, turning to look at her.

"Yes. What do you call it?"

Johnny didn't answer. He just turned back and pointed at the map at a city in the middle. "Is this city us?"

"Yes," Restaria replied.

Johnny pointed to a picture of a group of buildings to the South. "This is Balti-mor-ee."

"We call it Ballmor," Restaria said with a grim look, pointing her staff towards the map. "It is where the Krakn live. They are very fierce and terrible. One night they came from the sea and killed all they found. They ate them raw, and all who could get away escaped. There are still some men left in hiding in the city, doing their best to retake it, but it is a dangerous and risky task."

Starbucks and the others walked over to listen. Starbucks said, "We've met the Krakn. I would have to agree with that."

"The Krakn are moving North looking for more people to eat, towards us. Every day we have more and more fights with them.

"And to the North of Pelpia lies the city of Nork, another enemy we must contend with." Restaria pointed to another drawing on the map. "Nork is vast, and has many people and groups living there, as well as many strange creatures and monsters. A man they simply call the Boss reigns the streets with an iron hand. He calls himself the King of Nork.

"The Boss has sent spies south to watch us. He sent an army of Norkers, as they call themselves, down to supposedly barter with us, but I really feel they were here to size up our ability to defend ourselves. I fear he is also heading our way with soldiers to try and conquer us."

"Seems like there's always somebody looking for a fight," Deb said gloomily.

"Until Misterwizard reunites the people of the land under Mocracy, it's going to be that way," Johnny said.

"How did you manage to do so much in so little time, Restaria?" Deb asked.

Johnthebaptist, who stood nearby, piped in with pride. "Restaria is the smartest of all of us. Even when she was a scrabbler, she tried to learn the old words and fill her mind with knowledge. Now she leads us because she is all wise and knowing."

Johnny and his friends grinned at each other. "Oh, Misterwizard has got to meet her," Super said. They all nodded in agreement.

Restaria smiled. "We are yet a small community, but we grow bigger every day, and are training to defend ourselves. Perhaps your Misterwizard would be willing to make a pact with us. We could use some allies in our fight."

"Of course, he would!" Deb said, before Johnny could say it. "Our tribe is always looking for good people to join us and bring back what Johnny said, Mocracy."

Johnny chuckled. "Yes, Restaria, he would be glad

to. If we didn't have to find our lost friend, we would accompany you back to Washinton Deecee and introduce you to him right now."

"Perhaps we can send some people to meet him ourself."

"You should!" Starbucks said. "Just make sure you go way around Ballmor to get there."

They all laughed and Restaria led them outside again. They walked outside and to another building not far away, another brick building one-story high, adorned with skulls of men and animals, furs and shiny baubles. On the front was a large sign with a symbol none of them recognized. It showed what looked like two snake-beasties crawling up a pole.

"This is Arrex's lodge. He is our healer. He will help fix your friend's leg. When you are done here, we will bring you to the Great Hall, where you can have some food."

"Food sounds really good right now!" Starbucks said.

"Yes, sir," Deb added. Even Deecee seemed to understand what Restaria said, for he licked his lips and whined.

Starbucks turned to Johnny. "You three go and eat. Me and Super will join you after she's taken care of."

"Are you sure we should split up?" Johnny said.

"I think we're safe here, Johnny," Deb said. "For once."

They all grinned and nodded. Johnny, Deb and Deecee followed Restaria towards the Great Hall, and Starbucks and Super went into the Medicine Man's lodge. As they left, Johnny smiled. "It's nice to have a chance to relax, with no one trying to kill us."

"Amen to that!" Deb said, as they both laughed.

CHAPTER 12

Monsta and Lady Stabs drove up to the huge wall in front of Phill-a-delpia. Monsta stopped for a moment, just out of sight, and sat, the engine running.

"Someone has taken over our city."

"Johnny and his friends would have avoided this wall and went around."

Monsta turned in his seat and studied her, and Lady Stabs knew he suspected something. "Maybe we should find a way inside, just to make sure."

Lady Stabs shrugged. "If you want to get caught and let Johnny and his friends get further and further away."

Monsta studied her for a moment more as she held her breath, not sure if she was going to have to fight for her life at any moment.

Then he turned around again, and she sighed silently with relief.

"This city belongs to the Doomsday Prophecy. Once we are done with Johnny and strengthened our numbers, we will come back. We will kill everyone inside who has dared to try and take our place. Then the city will be ours again."

Monsta turned the Harley and slowly motored forward, to go around the wall. Lady Stabs knew if she wanted to survive, she had to find a chance to escape.

Suddenly in front of them, two men appeared with green vests and holding bows and arrows. They aimed their weapons at Monsta and Lady Stabs. One was tall and broad with a beard. The other man had yellow hair and a scar on his cheek.

The bearded man yelled, "Stop! Declare yourselves!"

Lady Stabs watched as Monsta scowled and gunned his engine, speeding towards the men. The bearded man shot his arrow and Lady Stabs screamed as it penetrated Monsta's shoulder. The Harley spun sideways and both Monsta and Lady Stabs were flung off. The Harley skittered away as the men ran up to them.

Monsta lay still, looking unconscious.

"Lay still, or we will shoot again!" The yellow haired man commanded.

Lady Stabs felt a pain in her side where she'd slid on the hard concrete, and she could tell she was bleeding there, but it was only a scrape. It would sting for a long time, but she knew it would heal. She lay still, her hands visible, waiting to see what the men would do.

Inside, Lady Stabs was pleased the men had stopped them, for the men didn't seem like they were evil, only protecting their land, and she'd been freed from Monsta, though not in the way she'd expected. She smiled grimly, wondering if she'd now have a chance to reunite with Johnny.

The men walked up warily; arrows pointed at them.

"You tried to ram us," the bearded man said gruffly. "We had no choice but to shoot."

"What are you doing sneaking around Pelpia?" The yellow-haired man said to Lady Stabs. "Speak, or we'll shoot you as well!"

Lady Stabs opened her mouth to speak, but suddenly Monsta struck. He was only pretending to be out. As Lady Stabs screamed, Monsta jumped up, knife in hand, and stabbed the closest man, the bearded one, in the chest. The other man's eyes went wide, and he backed up, trying to aim his arrow at Monsta.

Monsta, murder in his eyes, dropped the first man, who was already dead, and rushed toward the yellow-haired man. The yellow-haired man dropped his bow and arrow and ran away. Monsta chased him for a moment then, grinning darkly, turned and came hurrying back to Lady Stabs.

Lady Stabs had managed to get up, and she held a hand against her bloody side where the skin had been rubbed off. Her head felt woozy, and things were happening so fast, she was having trouble keeping up. Now she was back in Monsta's hands, and he'd killed the guard patrolling this new kingdom. The other one had run off, surely to get reinforcements. Now they would be lucky to escape with their lives, and the people of this land they called Pelpia would surely consider her an enemy. Things taken another turn, this time for the worse.

"Why didn't you help me?" Monsta yelled at her.

"It all happened so fast," Lady Stabs said, trying to think, her head spinning.

Monsta just glared at her and grunted. The arrow had stuck into his leather coat and only penetrated a tiny bit into his flesh. He pulled it out and snapped it angrily in his hands. He walked over to the body of the man he'd killed and glared down at him.

Monsta snorted. "If this is all they have defending this city, we will take it back easy. We'll be back, and then they'll pay."

"We should get out of here, before more come!" Lady Stabs said, really afraid that they would indeed be surrounded at any minute and both killed.

Monsta snorted again with haughty disdain and intentionally walked slowly over to the Harley. He picked it up off the ground and made a big show of examining it for damage.

Lady Stabs glared at him, wishing more than ever she could kick him in the butt and run away.

Finally, he climbed on and looked at her. Glumly she reluctantly walked over towards him. The last thing in the world she wanted to do was to get back on the Harley with Monsta, but it appeared as if once again, she had no choice.

Monsta didn't say anything, just turned the switch. The Harley roared to life. He gunned the engine once, twice, three times, just to show he wasn't afraid of being caught. Then he waited, not even looking at her as if making the point she had no choice. Lady Stabs climbed back on.

Monsta sped off and Lady Stab almost slipped but grabbed hold of him at the last second, her side stinging painfully and her vision blurry.

As they sped down a side street past the side of the wall again, Lady Stabs looked at it with a sense of longing and sadness. Johnny and Starbucks had been behind them, but they would surely go into this Pelpia when they arrived. Would the people of Letfreedomring welcome them, or capture them as well? Or were they inside, right now, enjoying a nice warm bed and a good meal? So far, she thought glumly, she wasn't doing a very good job of being their protector. Lady Stabs couldn't remember a time when she felt so all alone and vulnerable. She began to wish she'd stayed in New Sanctuary after all.

Johnny and Deb finished what turned out to be a very pleasant meal of deer-beastie meat and potatoes, with homemade grape juice to drink. Deecee sat on the floor, chewing on a deer-beastie bone, looking very happy. It was one of the best meals Johnny could remember, and he began to really like Restaria and the people of Letfreedomring.

Johnny looked at Deb, and she looked back at him. They laughed and gazed into each other's eyes. It struck Johnny again how beautiful Deb was, with her long blond hair, blue eyes, and cheerful smile, always ready to laugh. How lucky he was that she loved him!

Almost as if reading Johnny's thoughts, Deb took

his hand and leaned towards him. They stared at each other for a second, then Deb kissed him. Johnny felt the warmth of love rush through him as he felt her tender lips touching his, and he kissed her back hard. Suddenly Johnny wasn't thinking about the good food anymore, and Deb could tell. She pushed him away.

"Johnny better behave himself," she said, and they both chuckled. Behaving himself was the last thing Johnny wanted to do, but he knew she was right. He smiled at her and she grinned back, eyes twinkling.

Johnny sensed a presence and turned to see Restaria watching them from the back of the room. She'd seen what Johnny and Deb were doing and she smiled.

"I can see you two are very much in love. It is nice to see that again."

Deb blushed and Johnny just felt uncomfortable and frowned.

"Soon, I hope we will fill the land once again with people just like you, and the world will be a good place again."

"I hope so, Restaria," Johnny said. "Can you tell me how Super is? Is her leg better?"

Restaria nodded. "Yes. She is resting in a bed at our Place of Healing. Your friend Starbucks is with her. We have brought them some food there."

"Your food is wonderful," Deb said. "Thank you so much for sharing it."

Johnny stood up and walked over to Restaria

"Restaria, here in this city, our leader Misterwizard had a castle. We need to visit it so that we can get some supplies for our journey."

"Oh yes," Restaria said. "This place is a national shrine for us, for even before we heard of you and were a people, tales of Misterwizard ran through the wildies. He was always a mysterious and terrible magic man to be feared and revered. None can enter there, but you are course, are different. You can go there if you please."

Johnny and Deb walked outside with Deecee trotting along beside them to find the Harleys parked on the steps. Johnny turned to Deb.

"We need to bring the Harleys over to Misterwizard's castle. He has a special tank with the strange water in it that we need to make the Harleys run. Do you think you could ride Starbuck's over there?"

Deb hopped on Starbuck's Harley with an excited grin. "It's about time I got to drive one by myself!"

Johnny grinned and climbed on his Harley. He watched closely as Deb did all the things needed to make the Harley start. He was impressed.

"You did it all right!"

"Why are you so surprised, Johnny Apocalypse?"

Deb said tartly. "I've been watching you boys do it for a long time."

Johnny shrugged and laughed. "Ready to ride?"

"Let's go!" Deb said, roaring the engine.

Johnny started out slowly, watching Deb. Very slowly and wobbly at first, Starbuck's Harley started moving. Johnny was sure she was going to fall over, and a few times she tilted precariously, but soon she was driving along next to Johnny, wearing a big grin.

Soon they could see the spires of Misterwizard's castle in the distance. As they approached the castle, Johnny felt a feeling of joy, almost as if he was coming home. He remembered all the good times he'd had with Misterwizard there, the hours of learning and discovery with his old mentor. He hoped the Gangers hadn't destroyed too much of the wonderful things Misterwizard had inside.

They reached the fence to find it festooned with flowers and gifts, almost as if it was being worshiped. It still had the skulls and other frightening objects Misterwizard had adorned it with to scare away intruders as well. Johnny and Deb stopped and gazed at it, silently, both lost in their own thoughts.

Johnny climbed off his Harley, walked over to the gate and with a smile and a flourish yelled, "Open Sesame!"

As if by magic, the gate sprang open, just like it did before. He grinned at Deb. Deecee barked. Then Johnny slowly pulled the gate open and Deb drove inside. He hopped on his Harley and followed her.

The first thing Johnny did was find the special water for the Harleys and fill them up. Then he added an extra container of the water to the backs of the Harleys for future use. Then he and Deb walked to the front of Misterwizard's castle.

They reached the two huge doors leading to the main floor of Misterwizard's castle. Deb waited excitedly as Johnny swung the doors wide and they entered.

A rush of cold, stale air greeted them, and Deb shivered and hugged herself. Once more inside the giant hall, they gazed on all the amazing things Misterwizard had collected. There were cars and machines and statues and clothing. But this time, Johnny and Deb were dismayed to see so many of the glass cases smashed open and tables turned over. Some of the beautiful paintings had been slashed, a few of the statues had been tipped over so they broke into pieces.

Johnny looked at the mess with anger. Deb grabbed his arm and pulled him close.

"Don't worry Johnny, Misterwizard has lots more amazing things, and he can find new ones to replace the things the gangers broke."

Johnny nodded, trying to smile, but all he could do was lead Deb over to the stairs, so he didn't have to look at the destruction anymore.

They walked up the stairs in cool darkness, but Deb wasn't afraid this time. It was like coming home again. They reached the second floor and entered Misterwizard's room. Here there was less destruction, but items were strewn about and laying on the floor. Johnny and Deb picked up what they could and tried to clean up.

Johnny found an old book on the floor and he picked it up. He smiled as he gazed at it, for it brought back a wonderful memory.

"Look, Deb. Do you know what this says?"

Deb looked at the book with interest. The cover was faded and gray, but the faint image of what looked like a man with a very strange haircut was on the cover. There were only two words at the top. "Of course, I don't, smarty. Who's that strange man on the front?"

Johnny laughed. "It's not a man, it's a monkey-beastie. This book is called "Curos Gorg." It's one of the books Misterwizard taught me to read with. I'd sure like to take a lot of the stuff here back to Sanctuary so we could pass it on to—"

Johnny stopped, suddenly embarrassed at what he was about to say.

"I would too," Deb said, laughing at him. "And someday, maybe we can."

Johnny put the book down reluctantly and studied Misterwizard's maps for a while, while Deb messed around in Misterwizard's "kitchen." She found some green bottles filled with red liquid. She poured some in a glass and tasted it, and was very good, so she poured them both a glass. They sat sipping it and gazing out the windows at Pelpia beyond.

"We need to look for some of the special stuff Misterwizard had for Super's leg," Johnny said.

Deb nodded and pointed. "I saw some things over on that table in the corner. How are we going to know which one to use?"

Johnny hadn't really thought about that. If they gave Super the wrong stuff, it might do more harm than good.

"Maybe Restaria will know. We'll just take as much as we can back to Bell House and she can help us sort it out."

"That sounds smart," Deb said.

Suddenly Johnny realized that he and Deb were alone for the first time in a while. He looked at Deb, and she saw and looked back. She immediately could tell what he was thinking and smiled.

"Johnny needs to behave himself!"

"Why?" Johnny replied, and he put his arms around her. As she melted into his arms, he kissed her and for a few minutes they just enjoyed each other and being in love, and knowing they would always have each other.

Finally, Johnny brought himself around, remembering that there were people in danger waiting on them. As Deb watched, woozy, fixing her hair, he walked over and gathered as many 'medicins' as he could in a bag.

"Now that the Gangers are gone, we should make this our outpost," Johnny said. "I'm going to ask Restaria if we can use Misterwizard's castle as a place to stop when we go exploring."

Deb nodded "I'm sure she won't mind."

Suddenly Deb saw something out the window in the distance. A whole crowd of townspeople were running down the street, talking excitedly and looking upset.

"Look, Johnny! What do you think happened?"

"I don't know," Johnny replied, "but we'd better go find out."

They finished their drinks, gathered a few more supplies from Misterwizard's room and hurried back down the stairs to find out what had happened.

CHAPTER 13

Johnny and Deb ran back down the stairs with Deecee trotting along behind them, and out of Misterwizard's castle to find a crowd standing outside the gate. As they approached the gate, they saw a body lying on a wooden cart. All the people stood around it as a man with yellow hair talked excitedly in a loud voice.

Johnny and Deb looked at each other, both wondering what was going on. Just then, the crowd parted and Restaria walked up. The yellow-haired man began to talk to her excitedly, but he was too far away for Johnny and Deb to hear.

Johnny and Deb climbed back on their Harleys. Deecee jumped into his basket on Johnny's Harley and they rode to the gate. As Deb watched Johnny said, "Open Sesame!" and the gate sprang open. Johnny rode out with Deb right behind him. Then Johnny yelled the words again and the gate closed.

They rode to where the crowd stood in the middle of the street. When they arrived, Restaria was just done talking to the man and she turned towards them.

"Two of our guards caught a man and a woman on a machine much like yours outside the wall. The man killed one of our men and tried to kill the other, but he escaped. They rode off to the north towards Nork."

Johnny and Deb looked at each other. "Johnny," Deb said, "That means whoever he is, he's very dangerous. Lady Stabs must be his prisoner!"

Starbucks arrived, an arm around Super whose leg was bandaged.

"What'd we miss?" Starbucks said. "And what's Deb doing on my Harley?"

A little later, Johnny, Restaria and all of Johnny's friends sat inside Bell House. Super sat on a bench stroking Deecee's fur, who stood beside her. Johnny and Restaria faced each other. Johnny had given Restaria the medicines he found in Misterwizard's castle, and she was able to find one called "anti-biotic" that she gave to Super to take.

"Restaria, we would love to stay, but we need to find our friend before something bad happens to her."

Restaria looked at Johnny, then at his friends. She

smiled at Johnny. "I understand. Just know that if you travel to Nork, you are walking into a very dangerous realm. They do not like visitors."

"Which is exactly why we need to rescue our friend Lady Stabs!" Deb said.

"Johnny," Starbucks said, frowning, "I don't think Super should leave here. Her leg is still healing."

"I can too go!" Super said, frowning in protest and standing up. "I can do anything——"

Suddenly she stopped talking, winced in pain and sat down again, making the others smile.

"Sure, you can," Starbucks said. He turned to Johnny. "Maybe I should stay with her."

"No, Johnny needs you, Starbucks!" Deb said. "I'll stay with Super here in Letfreedomring. You two will go much faster without us, and you can sneak up on Lady Stab's capturer better with just two of you."

"I don't like it," Starbucks scowled, not liking that idea at all. It became obvious to the others that Starbucks was missing some time alone with Super too. They all secretly smiled.

Johnny walked over to Starbucks, grinning. "I know you want to stay here with Super, Starbucks, and I don't blame you. And I'm going to miss Deb. But I think she's right. The two of us will have much better luck catching up to Lady Stabs than four of us."

Starbucks nodded glumly, not happy, but knowing they were right. "Are you sure you're going to be okay here alone, Super?"

"She won't be alone; I'll be with her!" Deb said crossly.

"I think I'll leave Deecee here to keep them company too. It will be easier for us to make ground without him."

"It's like we're breaking up," Starbucks said.

Super stood up again and hobbled over to Starbucks. She put her hands on his cheeks and as everyone watched with amusement, kissed him deeply. When she was done, Starbucks looked woozy with a big grin on his face.

"I know you're going to miss me, Stupid. I'm going to miss you, too. So, hurry up and find Lady Stabs and come back, so I can give you a nice, friendly welcome back."

They all laughed.

"I love you, you silly little scrabbler." Super said.

"I love you too, silly girl," Starbucks answered back. Then they kissed.

Johnny turned to Deb expectantly. "Don't I get a kiss goodbye too?"

As they all laughed again, Deb ran over, put her arms around Johnny's neck and gave him a good kiss.

Then with her arms still around his neck they gazed at each other with happy smiles.

"I'm going to miss you too, Johnny. And I love you, but you already know that. Just be careful. You know what will happen to me if I ever lose you."

Johnny's face betrayed the deep emotions running through him. "You'll never lose me, Little Debbie, because I love you more than anything in the world. And this is the last time I'm going to be separated from you, if I have anything to say about it."

Monsta rode fast, his long black hair flowing in the wind. Lady Stabs held onto him and tried not to think how every mile was taking them further and further away from her friends.

The road seemed to go on forever, with no end. They passed by old houses, mostly piles of sticks with dark, haunted interiors. Occasionally she would spy a shadow in one of them, a figure, someone lurking inside. Every time it sent a chill up her spine. The world seemed so dangerous now; everyone was an enemy waiting to attack or kill you.

She rebuked herself for thinking such things

because they weren't true. She'd found lots of good people in Johnny and his tribe, and even the Undergrounders. But there did seem to be just as many bad people as good.

Suddenly they began passing an area of pure desolation. The houses disappeared and all around was flat, black ground. Off on their right, there was not even a tree or anything living. She stared open mouthed, fascinated.

"Look, Monsta."

Monsta glanced over and kept riding, in fact he sped up. "This place where Mushroom Monster came. Must get away fast, bad magic here."

As they sped along, Lady Stabs saw one thing standing in the vast emptiness. It was a fence made of some kind of metal you could see through. It ran along all by itself on the scorched black grass. Leaning crazily one away from them in one place and towards them in another. It looked lonely somehow, like it was still trying to do its job and keep things out, but it couldn't because there was nothing left to protect, and it had fallen down in places. Lady Stabs looked at the ground and saw what looked like a gate. On the gate was a piece of wood with some writing on it. The words said, "McGuire Air Force Base" and below them it said, "Force Condition Delta." Lady Stabs wished Johnny were around to tell her what it said. Maybe he could tell her what had been there, and why the Mushroom Monsters wanted to destroy it.

Lady Stabs thought about Monsta. The way he drove so fast, she began to wonder if he really didn't care if he found Johnny anymore, just wanted to find a place to make a new start. And he thought she liked him and would start it with him. She had to make him keep thinking that, until she could find a way to escape. The thought of being trapped with him for a lifetime somewhere in the middle of nowhere with no way to escape was too horrible to contemplate. He was a brutish, cruel, savage man with no human compassion, and every moment she was with him, she detested it more.

It grew late. The red eye sank over the distant hills. Soon Lady Stabs knew the yellow eye would open. She wondered if Monsta would stop for the night. She felt so tired, she desperately hoped so. She didn't know how long she could hold onto him and not simply fall asleep and off the Harley.

Suddenly Monsta looked up and stopped the Harley, and Lady Stabs looked up to see why.

Monsta stared into the distance, looking at something. Lady Stabs followed his gaze, and then she saw it too. On the horizon like a vision, tall buildings shot up into the sky like giant fingers reaching to the sky, as if trying to touch the stars. There were hundreds of them. They seemed to go on forever, some taller and some shorter, but all right next to each other like soldiers standing at attention. It was like a forest, but not of trees, of buildings. How could they ever make so many buildings? How many people must have lived there to fill all of them? The sheer number awed and scared Lady Stabs, and yet a thrill of discovery filled her. This was a new and fascinating place. She just wished she could have seen it first with her friends, not with an enemy.

But then she saw there was something strange about the buildings too. It was too far to see clearly yet, but there was something attached to them. Whatever it was, it looked creepy and reminded her of something that filled her with a sense of dread, as if it was something they definitely shouldn't get close to. But she knew no matter how much she protested, Monsta wouldn't care. He was too dumb to avoid danger.

Who lived amongst all those tall buildings, she wondered? Surely many people lived there, and who knew what other creatures. It was foolish to go there, dangerous, for whoever did surely wouldn't like strangers. But she knew Monsta would go and blindly lead the into danger, without a consideration for what happened to her, in fact he'd surely use her for bait if he needed to. Anger and desperation filled her. She had to get away before he dragged her there. Somehow, she knew something terrible was going to happen to her if she journeyed to those tall, strange buildings and the strange something that covered them.

"We shouldn't go there," she said, voicing her thoughts and hoping Monsta would listen, though she doubted it. "We don't know who's down there!"

Monsta just laughed and started the Harley again, but suddenly they heard sounds. It was the voices of men and a chorus of other strange noises… squeaking?

Something was heading right for them, and it sounded like a whole army.

CHAPTER 14

Somewhere in front of them, a loud melodic tune echoed in the air. And mixed with it were the strangest sounds.

"Is that squeaking?" Lady Stabs said.

Before Monsta could reply over the rise in front of them came an amazing, unbelievable sight. Men in ragged striped suits and wearing hats with wide brims rode up, hundreds of them, a whole army. Most held clubs or swords or sharp sticks, but a few seemed to have some sort of gun or rifle. But it was what they rode on that amazed and terrified Monsta and Lady Stabs.

Giant rat-beasties! As big as horse-beasties, with saddles and rope bridles, covered with gray fur and with creepy pink feet. Their sharp teeth and beady black eyes made them look like something out of a nightmare. They had bridles on their noses and saddles on their backs and the men yanked on the reigns constantly to keep them under control.

The men had trouble controlling them for every few minutes one of the rat-beasties would rise up on its hind legs and sniff the air or try to run off to the side. The man riding it would beat it with a club until it settled down and started scampering ahead again in short spurts. At the head of the rat-beastie procession, one man sat on a rat-beastie. He held a small silver box the size of a man's hand up to his mouth and moved it back and forth, and from it came the melody they heard.

The rat-beasties ran fast, like a horrible moving gray carpet. In seconds they would overtake Monsta and Lady Stabs.

Lady Stabs felt her blood run cold and her skin crawl. She grew so scared she felt faint. Monsta just stared, open-mouthed. "What kind of beasties are those?"

Lady Stabs squeezed his arm. "I don't know, but let's get out of here!"

Monsta tried to turn the Harley around and do just that. But before he could even get going, the men and their rat-beasties overtook them.

Soon they were surrounded by the rat-beasties and their riders, who crowded in next to them, moving wall of gray, hairy monsters. Lady Stabs screamed as one of them nipped at her. She shrank back against Monsta, who looked scared himself. The smell of the creatures was horrible, and some of them had scars from some sort of battle. The rat-beasties tried to run in different directions or rear up and the men beat them to keep them under control.

One of the men in the front looked like the leader. He wore a nicer black suit with gold stripes and a black hat with a band on it. His rat-beastie had a fancy gold blanket under its saddle. He rode up and blocked Monsta's path. He held a strange rifle with a round disc in the middle of it. He pointed it at Monsta's chest.

"Freeze, Cinderella, and reach for the sky, or I'll drill you with my Tommy gun."

Monsta and Lady Stabs glanced at each other in puzzlement and then back at the man. The man pulled up on the reigns of his rat, which raised up on its haunches and squeaked in protest. Then it dropped back down as the man climbed off. He walked up to Monsta and pointed his gun at him.

"Make like a statue, or I'll ventilate ya. Kapish?"

Monsta didn't understand a word them man said. He simply glared at the man in hatred, but he didn't move. It was obvious the man had the drop on him.

The man looked Lady Stab up and down with a quizzical look, as if he couldn't figure out what she was.

Then he studied Monsta.

"You   escape   from   the   circus?" The other men on their rats chuckled.

"What are ya, stupid or somethin'?"

Monsta and Lady Stabs just sat there, not sure what to think or do.

The man smiled, having fun with his teasing. He looked at Monsta's Harley. "Hey, that's some nice chopper ya got there. I always wanted one like that. How you get it to run? We got stuff like that all over Nork, but we could never figure it out how to make 'em work. Most of 'em are so beat-up they're nothing but piles a' junk."

Monsta just glared back, not answering. The man looked back at another guy on a rat-beastie right next to him who looked like his second in command. This man didn't look as fancy as the leader, but he looked better than most of the others.

"Hey Bugsy, ain't that a nice chopper?"

"Yeah, sure is, Moxie," Bugsy said. "I think you should take it. He ain't gonna need it no more."

Monsta snarled, "You touch my Harley and I'll kill you. You freaks better get out of our way!"

This didn't create the reaction Monsta hoped, for all the men just laughed even harder, especially the leader. It seemed they knew perfectly well who had the upper hand.

"Oh, tough guy, eh? Well, we'll see how tough you are tough guy when I fill ya full of holes." Moxie walked up and with the butt of his gun, hit Monsta on the chin. Lady Stabs screamed as Monsta flew off his Harley and landed on the ground. The action made the rat-beasties around get agitated, and the men beat them back into submission. Monsta lay on the ground and looked up, dazed and bloody. Moxie walked up and stared down at him with menace.

"Maybe you just learned somethin.' You got some nerve heading towards Nork like you was on a Sunday stroll. Now it's gonna cost ya. But you're lucky. We're on our way to a hit, so ya bought yourself some time. Meanwhile, you keep your kisser clamped shut and ya act like an angel, if you know what's good for ya."

Moxie pointed to Lady Stabs. "You, sweetheart, climb off, and I mean pronto."

Lady Stabs obeyed and stood silently, nervously eyeing the giant rat-beasties around her. One wiggled its whiskers and opened and closed its mouth showing sharp, pointed teeth. Lady Stabs felt sure it was going to nip at her at any second.

Moxie pointed to another man, a thin, tall, nervous looking guy with a long nose and a narrow face on a small rat-beastie. "Charlie, she rides with you."

Charlie smiled, showing two missing front teeth, looking happy at the thought. "You got it Moxie. We gonna have fun together, baby, you and me."

Moxie motioned towards Charlie. Lady Stabs reluctantly walked over to Charlie's rat-beastie. She eyed it with fright, and Charlie grinned. "Don't worry. He ain't gonna bite ya. Unless'en he's hungry."

The other men laughed.

"Just keep your hands away from his mouth. He likes to nip."

With disgust, Lady Stabs climbed on behind Charlie, trying not to think about what she was doing or breathe in the horrible smell so she wouldn't get sick and throw up. She had a feeling her new captors wouldn't like that very much.

Moxie motioned to Monsta with his gun, who lay on the ground, staring daggers at him.

"You joker, get to walk. Up and at 'em."

Monsta stood up, fuming. "What about my Harley?"

"You mean my Harley, Stupid."

The others all laughed again.

Monsta could barely contain himself. He balled up his fists and said through clenched teeth, "You just wait. You ain't always gonna have all your freak friends around."

Moxie's eyes opened wide for a second, but then he recovered, and he grinned. "Listen to this guy, will ya? He don't learn very well."

They all chuckled again.

Suddenly one of the rat-beasties rose on its hind legs. The man riding it fell off and the rest of the men around it jumped off their rat-beasties and ran to try and control it.

As Monsta laughed and Lady Stabs stared in horror, the rat-beastie bit its former rider on the side and the man screamed. The man standing around it shot it with their tommy-guns, making a rat-a-tat sound. It only seemed to make the rat-beastie angrier. It turned, grabbed one of the men in its sharp, white teeth and lifted him in the air. As he screamed, it flung him away like a rag doll. Finally, after shooting at it for a long time, the rat-beastie finally fell over on its side, dead.

Moxie walked over, looking irritated. Monsta laughed and said in a mocking tone, "You guys are the stupidest I've ever seen. Riding rat-beasties! And wearing those goofy outfits. You sure don't control them very well."

The other men smiled, knowing how Moxie was gonna react and what was coming. Moxie walked over to Monsta took out a metal ring from is pocket, put it on is hand and slugged Monsta in the midsection. Monsta yelled, "oof!" and slumped over, his hand on his stomach.

Moxie grinned with pleasure as the other men chuckled. He took his brass knuckles off and dropped them back in his pocket. "That's a lesson for ya. Keep your trap shut. Nobody can really control a ratty, but that's part of the deal. They're good for intimidatin.' And they're also good in battle, which shows what little a mug like you knows. And don't ever make fun of our suits again, or I'll knock yer teeth out. When I'm done with you, I'm gonna feed you to one of our rattys. What do you think of that, wise guy?"

Moxie walked away as Monsta stared after him. Lady Stabs called to Monsta from where she sat on the rat-beastie.

"You shouldn't antagonize them if we ever want to get away!"

Monsta scoffed, but Lady Stabs could tell when he spoke that fear hid behind his words. "He ain't always gonna have his friends. And I'm gonna kill him one day."

Charlie, sitting in front of Lady Stabs, pointed with his pistol. "Get up and start marching, sweetheart, or you die right here and now, and all your palaver wit you."

Monsta reluctantly got up. Moxie told one of his men to walk the Harley next to them, a spoil of war. The men on their rat-beasties began moving again, Moxie in the lead, towards Pelpia.

"Please, will you tell me where you're taking us?" Lady Stabs asked Charlie over his shoulder.

Charlie glanced back at her with a look of pride. "We're gonna put the hit on Pelpia. We did a recon a couple months back, and now we's ready to exact some tribute."

Moxie looked over from his mount and glared at him, and Charlie looked scared.

"Whazza matter with you? You got spangoli for brains?"

Charlie shrugged. Moxie put up a hand and pulled on his reins, making his rat-beastie stop. The rest of the army stopped too. He looked at Lady Stabs.

"It don't really matter, anyway. Thanks to knucklehead over there, you ain't going there now." Moxie turned to Charlie. "Charlie, you and Ticktock take these two jokers back to Nork. Show 'em to the Boss. He'll decide what to do with 'em."

"But I want to be in on the action!" Charlie groused.

"Me too!" Ticktock, a big black man, in a purple suit said He was so big he was bursting out of it and the arms and legs stuck out. The suit wouldn't close on him and the black shirt he wore underneath showed through. He wore a one of the nicest hats, though, a white one with a purple band and shiny black boots. His rat-beastie seemed to be the only one that didn't try to misbehave, probably out of fear.

"You're too stupid to be in on it, Charlie," Moxie said. "And ya don't deserve to, after runnin' yer mouth. Ticktock, you're sharp enough to keep these two from tryin' anything."

Ticktock smiled at the compliment, slightly mollified. Charlie scowled.

"Get the lead out. We got a war to fight. But wait a minute."

Moxie climbed off his rat-beastie. He grinned with desire and walked over to the Harley.

"Leave that alone! That's mine!" Monsta yelled, his face turning red.

"It's actually mine," Lady Stabs said, but no one heard her or listened.

Moxie walked over and climbed on the Harley. He looked it over with happy joy, like a scrabbler with its first toy.

"This is real nice." Moxie looked it over some more and turned some buttons, pushed on the hand brake.

Monsta snorted with mocking laughter. "You don't even know how to ride one!"

Moxie's face colored, and he scowled at Monsta

with dark fury. Monsta quickly realized he may have crossed over the line, and he quieted down.

Charlie tried not to grin, but Ticktock didn't, he grinned wide, showing white teeth. "You better off staying on your ratty, Moxie," Ticktock said, chuckling. "That thing looks dangerous."

Moxie glared at Monsta. "Get over here and teach me, real fast, or the first thing I'm gonna do is use it to drag your body around Nork."

Monsta grumbled to himself and walked over. "Pull that lever there with your hand. Push that button."

Moxie did what Monsta said, and a familiar rumble erupted from the bowels of the Harley. Moxie grinned big. "Hey, I'm gonna like this. I'm ridin' in style!"

All the men of the army sat on their rat-beasties and chuckled. Moxie looked at Charlie. "All right, stop standing around with those silly grins. You and Ticktock get moving back to Nork. And take my ratty with ya. I got a better ride now."

Charlie grumbled and turned his rat-beastie around, heading back towards Nork. Ticktock tied Moxie's rat-beastie to his. Then he glared at Monsta. "Get moving, bud. I ain't one to mess with."

Monsta studied Ticktock. Even though Monsta was big, Ticktock looked even a little bigger. Monsta knew if he had to tangle with the gangster, he'd be in for a real fight. He decided for now he'd obey, until he saw his chance. He sullenly started walking. Ticktock and his rat-beastie pulled in behind him and followed. The strange group heading away from the even stranger looking army, back in the direction Monsta and Lady Stabs had been heading in the first place.

Lady Stabs' mind filled with worry and unhappiness. Johnny and his friends had a war coming and there was nothing she could do to warn them. Meanwhile, she was prisoner, heading to who knew what fate. She knew she really had to escape now, or Johnny and his friends wouldn't know what was coming.

CHAPTER 15

Johnny and Starbucks took off in a squeal of tires and soon sped down the highway, leaving Bell House far behind. They soon came to the bridge Johnny and his friends crossed so long ago, the first time Johnny and Starbucks had taken the girls out of Sanctuary. Somewhere beyond it lay their old home.

Without a word, they both stopped and stared at it, remembering. The world around them was silent, almost as if it had paused for their moment of reflection. Starbucks looked over at Johnny. "Should we stop and check Sanctuary out, Johnny?"

Johnny looked thoughtful, feeling tumbling around inside him. "It would be nice to see the old place one more time, but I don't think we should stop. We need to find Lady Stabs. We have no idea how much distance they've already put between us."

Starbucks nodded. "Where do you think we should look?"

Johnny turned the throttle and slowly rolled away. "Anywhere on the way to Nork," Johnny said. Starbucks nodded and started moving again, and soon they were speeding along again.

"How long should we keep looking, Johnny?" Starbucks yelled over the roar of the engines.

Johnny thought about it. "A couple of days, at least. I don't want to leave the girls for too long, even though they seem safe right now."

Starbucks nodded. "Sounds good."

They drove along the river and on the other side, Johnny saw the funny building with the red bird on it. Johnny's mind replayed the day when the Gangers attacked and he herded the tribe to this building, before they set off on their great adventure. The images and memory filled Johnny with a feeling of quiet joy at having saved the Tribe, but also a strange sense of sadness, as if he was looking at a world long passed away.

To their right in the distance across the river lay the buildings of Sanctuary, just visible in the distance. Across the sea of concrete, the one-story buildings somehow looked sinister now. Here and there, burn marks ran up the outside of the walls, silent testimony to the deadly battle that occurred inside. They both knew what the other was thinking, how they both somehow missed Sanctuary, even though it was a dark prison, and how much they'd like to stop and just see what it looked like now. But neither said a word, just kept riding, silently lost in their own thoughts.

Soon they left Sanctuary behind and continued down the concrete ribbon that led between the buildings, and it wasn't long before they could no longer seen their old home. They kept riding, occasionally seeing wildies peering at them from the doorways of broken-down houses and buildings. Johnny wondered if they were part of Letfreedomring or were still alone.

They reached the south wall, and on top of it were more guards. At the base of the wall stood another gate, like the other one made of wood and old steel. From this side, Johnny could see it had a wooden beam across the middle set in two chocks, one on either side. The men manning the wall saw them coming and turned to look at them.

"Halt!" One of the men named Stop said, pointing his spear at them from the top of the wall.

Starbucks turned to Johnny. "This guy didn't get the message."

Johnny grinned. "The men guarding are always the last to hear anything."

Johnny called up to Stop. "We are friends of

Letfreedomring. We have met your leader Restaria and she allowed us to travel on. We are searching for a friend, a woman in a leather jacket riding a Harley like ours. She was with a man. Have you seen them? "

Stop rubbed his scratchy beard and thought. "No one like that has passed this way. But how do we know what you speak is the truth?"

"This is the great Johnny Apocalypse!" Starbucks said.

Stop's eyes widened, as did those of his men. "The Johnny Apocalypse?"

"Yes, and the lady we are talking about was kidnapped. We have to find her before something bad happens to her."

Stop motioned to his men and they opened the gate.

"Good luck, Johnny Apocalypse. I hope you find the friend you seek."

Johnny and Starbucks waved in thanks and rode out. Behind them the gate slammed shut. They were on their own again, heading into unknown territory.

After a little while the houses and buildings stopped and they found themselves riding down a much bigger ribbon of gray, this one divided into two sides with a metal railing between them. Here there was nothing but old rusted cars, pointing all different directions, as if a giant was playing with them and left them where they were when he was done.

The ribbon of concrete went on and on, seeming to have no ending, and after a while, Johnny, and Starbucks both began to feel uneasy and alone. They were so far from their friends and family, in a foreign land, not sure where they were going or what lay ahead. Neither said anything, just kept riding silently, weaving between cars.

Suddenly they heard something very strange ahead. It was the sound of tramping feet and the voices of men yelling. It sounded like an army, and it came from right in front of them!

"Hurry!" Johnny said. "Let's get off the road!"

They drove off the ribbon of concrete and behind a large tree on the side of the road.

And just in time. As they watched, an amazing and terrifying sight came into view. A few hundred men came riding towards them, a giant terrible army. But it was what they were riding that made them even more terrifying: giant rat-beasties!

Johnny and Starbucks stared, for they had never seen anything like it before. Being careful not to make a sound, they watched the army pass by. The men what looked like cloth suits, but most were ragged and looked like nothing but rags. Most of them had hats with brims on them. They all carried swords, sticks, clubs, or guns.

The rat-beasties squeaked and gnashed their fangs as the men controlled them with the ropes tied to the creatures' noses. Sometimes a rat-beastie would get out of control and a man would yank hard on the rope or beat it with his fist until it would settle down again.

"Johnny, who are they?"

Johnny stared at the strange army. Hideous and frightening, there was still something fascinating about the site of so many weird creatures being ridden by men.

"I don't know, Starbucks. I wonder if they are from Nork."

Finally, the last of the army passed by, and it was quiet again, as if they had never been there.

"If Lady Stabs and her captor ran into them, I feel sorry for them," Starbucks said glumly. "They're probably dead."

Then with dread Johnny realized something.

"Starbucks, they're headed for Pelpia!"

Starbucks turned to Johnny. "They're going to attack it!"

"The girls are there!" Johnny yelled.

"And Deecee! And Super is hurt!" Starbucks replied

Johnny started his Harley again. "We have to get back there fast!"

"What about Lady Stabs?" Starbucks asked. "And how? They're on the road we came on. There's no way we can get back in time any other way."

"We'll stay on the other side of them. They're on those weird rat-beasties. We should be able to ride right past them before they have time to do anything."

Starbucks started his Harley and they turned back towards Pelpia.

"And Lady Stabs?" Starbucks said, looking at Johnny.

Johnny looked regretful. "I know. I'm torn as well. But we have to think of Deb and Super now and warn Restaria and Letfreedomring."

"Yeah. I understand. I don't see much choice either. I'm afraid poor Lady Stabs is going to have to survive on her own, at least until we can pick up her trail again."

Johnny nodded. Both looked somber and sad as they took off, heading back the way they came, leaving Lady Stabs to her fate.

From the wall of Pelpia, Stop and the guards heard a strange roaring somewhere out in the darkness.

Stop peered out, his hand over his eyes. "What's that sound?"

Out of the darkness a lone figure rode forth on a strange, metal vehicle. Then suddenly as they watched, the strange vehicle tipped over and the man fell to the ground a hundred yards out from the wall.

Stop and the others looked at each other and smiled, then chuckled. Then they looked back. Their smiles turned to looks of horror.

From behind the man came creatures, hundreds of them. The creatures had beady black eyes and long, furry noses. They had little pink feet and whiskers that twitched. And they were all huge, the size of horse-beasties. Men rode on them, evil, cruel looking men.

The horrid gray army scampered towards them, silent on their little feet, making them seem even more terrifying. They filled the whole landscape, scurrying like a sickening gray moving carpet. They stopped when they reached the man and his strange machine as he struggled to get up and lift the machine off the ground.

A twenty-season old round and short man named Roadkill next to Stop said in a hushed tone full of amazement and fright, "Look at the monsters!"

Another man, older and gray-haired named Exit wailed, "They're from Nork! They've come back, and this time to kill us all!"

The rat-beasties rose on their hind legs and all squeaked at once, filling the air with an evil shrieking. The men on the wall covered their ears in pain.

Moxie, the man with the strange vehicle, left it standing on its kickstand and walked up until he was close enough to yell up to the men on the wall. He grinned and looked cocky and tough. "You mugs, up there on that wall!"

Stop yelled back, trying to sound angry and unafraid, but his voice was raspy and frail. "Who are you to approach the city of Pelpia? This is the land of the Letfreedomering. State your business or depart!"

"I'll state my bizness all right. You tell that boss lady of yours we wasn't too happy with the way you treated us last time. So, me and the Ratpack is here to pay a little social visit. This is your last chance to negotiate, sweetheart, and pay us tribute. You get yer boss and bring 'em here for a little heart to heart. Savvy?"

Stop looked confused, and he and Roadkill had a whispered consultation. Moxie looked annoyed. "HEY! Get your boss, got it, lame brain?"

Stop and Roadkill stopped arguing and turned to look at Moxie. "We are the people of Letfreedomring. This is our land!"

Moxie grinned, then chuckled. He turned and

mugged for his army. "This guy ain't too bright." They all laughed. "He says it's their land."

All of the men in the army laughed louder. Some shot their guns in the air. The rat-beasties grew agitated and fussed, but the men struggled with them until they got them under control again.

Moxie turned around, still grinning, and looked back at Stop and Roadkill. "Well, that's something that has yet to be determined, ain't it? Now go get yer boss, or you want we should just come in and find 'em for ourselves?"

"I'll get the boss!" Stop said in a panic. This made Moxie and the Norkers laugh again.

Stop turned to Roadkill. "Hurry! Get Restaria! We are under attack! Tell her to bring the army before it's too late!!"

Roadkill nodded, his head bobbing like a marionette, and jumped down off the wall on his short legs. He fell to the ground, rolled around for a second then hopped up and skittered off as fast as he could.

Stop turned to Exit and the other men. "We have to stall them until the army arrives!"

Exit shook his head and his gray beard waggled back and forth. "How? We're doomed!"

CHAPTER 16

ack at the place that used to be called Independence Hall but was now Bell House, Restaria's mayr room, Restaria sat in her executive chair talking to Deb and Super as they ate sandwiches. Deecee lay quietly next to them, his head on his paws. Deb and Super had just finished telling her about their adventures up to leaving Washington Deecee.

"Wonderful!" Restaria said smiling with pleasure. I must say, for such young girls, you have had an exciting life. The battles you've been in, and that strange story about the Undergrounders!"

"It was pretty exciting, that's for sure," Deb said.

"And the best part is, the Gangers are gone for good." Super said. She broke off a bit of her sandwich and fed it to Deecee, who gobbled it down happily.

"I now sincerely look forward to meeting your

Misterwizard and joining our people together in harmony. It is so encouraging to know we are not alone." Restaria turned to Super. "How is your leg, young lady?"

Super stood up and walked on her leg gingerly. "It's getting better. I can walk on it now if I don't put too much pressure on it."

"I can't wait to meet your tribe. I hope they will be happy to meet us."

"Of course, they will be!" Super said. "The only problem is, between us and you guys are those weird monsters in Ballmore."

"The Krakn," Restaria said, getting up and looking at the map. "It would be nice if we could find a way to find peace with those creatures as well, but I suspect that will not be the case. I'm afraid we will end up having to fight them and drive them back into the sea."

"We need to do something, so our two tribes can unite," Deb said. "Having an enemy between us is going to make it very difficult."

"You sound like Johnny!" Super said.

Suddenly Roadkill burst into the room, exhausted and panting, covered in sweat. He fell on the floor in a heap as Restaria and the girls jumped up in surprise.

"Who's he?" Super said.

Restaria ran over and knelt next to him. Two of her guards ran up. She turned to them. "Hurry, get Arrex.

This man is hurt!"

Roadkill turned and looked up at her. "The army from Nork is back! And this time they're riding monsters! They're going to attack!"

As the yellow eye rose in the night sky, the lone Krakn walked back to the ruins of Ballmor. It stopped in the middle of the street, in front of the first tall buildings and gazed up at them, searching with its large, oblong black eyes.

It waved its tentacles and then screeched, the sound shrill and piercing in the still evening air. It stopped and waited, but only silence greeted it. It called again; this time louder, more urgent.

Slowly from the floors of the buildings in front of it and the streets around, more of the black monsters appeared. The creature, encouraged, screeched again, louder, waving its tentacles around. Soon ten, twenty, thirty Krakn surrounded it, and more kept coming.

Then the larger, fiercer Krakn, the leader with his golden bands, appeared on the street to the left. The others moved out of its way and watched it as it approached the lone caller. It moved up to stand next to it. The lone caller looked frightened for a second by the giant creature that dwarfed it, but then its expression turned to one of dark excitement.

The leader waved its arms and screeched at it. The lone explorer screeched back. Then it turned and pointed towards Pelpia. It turned back and screeched some more.

The leader's eyes showed dark pleasure. It nodded its head and the lone creature smiled; its huge mouth full of razor-sharp teeth curving upwards.

The leader turned to the others and screeched, waving its arms. The others in unison screeched back, their voices excited, waving their tentacles too. The noise filled the air with deafening sound.

The leader turned to the loner and nodded. The loner turned and walked the way it had come, back towards Pelpia. But now, the leader and all the other Krakn followed.

Johnny and Starbucks hurried back towards Pelpia, and soon they saw the wall ahead of them. The red eye had disappeared, and the yellow eye rose from the distant hills to take its place in the night sky. In front of the wall as far as they could see, the rat-beastie army stood, squeaking and yelling, looking even creepier in the darkness.

Johnny and Starbucks stopped far enough away where they couldn't be seen and gazed at the frightening sight.

"It looks like we're too late," Starbucks said. "They're reached Pelpia!"

"It doesn't look like they've gotten inside yet," Johnny said. "If we circle around, maybe we can find a gate where they'll let us in."

Starbucks nodded and they rode again, careful to go slow to keep the sounds of their engines low. They drove to the right, careful to keep houses and buildings between them and the army. They weaved around old junk cars and trash and through overgrown strips of grass. Sometimes they had to fight around rickety old fences. Finally, they made their way to the wall on the side of the city. They drove for a while, then Starbucks saw something and pointed.

"Look, Johnny! I see an opening!"

Johnny looked where Starbucks pointed, and he saw what Starbucks was looking at. The wall was haphazardly constructed, and in places gaps appeared between the old rusted cars. In one place it leaned forward and looked ready to collapse. A street ran up to the wall and disappeared beneath it. To the right of the street, next to an old blue metal box, a small gap could be seen between an old yellow bus and a little orange car that looked like a dead ladybug-beastie. The opening was large enough for a man to sneak through, and maybe even a rat-beastie.

"The wall here is worse than the one we built at New Sanctuary," Johnny said as he frowned with disapproval.

"It sure is," Starbucks said. "If that army sees this, nothing is gonna stop them."

"Come on!" Johnny said. He rode his Harley down the street to the wall and then over to the gap. Starbucks followed.

Stopping their Harleys, they climbed off. Johnny positioned his so the gap was hidden behind it. Starbucks placed his close to help hide the opening too.

"Let's go find the girls," Johnny said. "Then we have to find a way to help Restaria and Letfreedomring fight."

"Man, it's always something," Starbucks said, grinning and shaking his head as the boys knelt down and crawled through the hole.

Restaria, Deb and Super listened with mounting horror as Roadkill, panting and stopping every few seconds to catch his breath, described the terrifying sight of the men on the rat-beasties attacking. As she listened, Restaria's face grew more and more grave. As they listened to his story, the crowd around them began to talk and murmur with fear. The word spread from one person to the next, and soon everyone in the building was talking loudly. It quickly spread outside and to the people nearby.

Restaria raised a hand to quiet the crowd so she could here, and the noise died down slightly.

Roadkill looked frightened as he talked on. "The guy in front said funny things just like last time, palaver, and savvy. He said we need to pay tribute, the Rat Pack was here. We didn't understand, but we got the idea he wants to talk to you."

Super looked at Restaria quizzically. "Tribute?"

Restaria looked at Deb and Super and nodded somberly. "Yes. They said something about that kind of thing when they were here before, just hinting at it. It was one of the reasons we were sure they were not there to be friends."

"You have to call up your army!" Deb said.

"Your people are going to have to fight," Super said.

Restaria replied. "Yes," But she looked less than

confident. She turned to one of her guards. "Ring the Bell and assemble the people. Tell Lightpole what has happened and tell him I said to gather the army. Tell him I am going to talk to their leader.!"

The man nodded and ran up the stairs towards the rope for the bell in Bell House.

Restaria walked out, with Deb, Super and Deecee following behind. It was night now, and the yellow eye was just rising behind the distant hills. A chill filled the air, making the women shiver and the danger seem even scarier.

They hurried down the street, and already all around them the word was being passed. An excitement and fear began to fill the air, as people were told about the invading army and ran to tell others. A crowd began to follow them, men and women carrying torches held high and clubs and sticks. They poured out of the buildings on either side of the highway, and soon the street was filled with anxious people.

Super hurried to keep up, Deecee staying next to her, and she seemed to be walking fairly well with only a slight limp. Suddenly in the distance behind them they heard the bell ringing out. Before a cheerful sound, it now filled the three women with a feeling of dread, knowing what it meant.

"Do you think your army will be able to fight them

off?" Super asked.

"I'm afraid calling what we have an army is generous," she said, looking grim. "We are small, only having begun to rebuild. The leader of our army is called Lightpole. He is a courageous man with a heart of steel, and he tries his best, but he had no real knowledge of war or battle tactics. He mainly has the men marching around and pretending to fight enemies. We have only a few hundred men at most, and we are only armed with clubs, bows and arrows and makeshift weapons."

"Not much against this terrible army," Super said somberly.

"Yes," Restaria replied. "Their city is much bigger than ours. We will do what we can, but our best plan of action may be to put up a brave front while our people find a way to escape to a place of safety."

"Abandon your home?" Deb asked.

Restaria nodded. "We may have no choice."

"You could always join us at New Sanctuary!" Super said. "I know they'd be happy to have you."

Restaria frowned. "I don't want to leave our home, give up what we are building here, but maybe it would only be until we can find a way to fight and get it back."

They reached the north wall leading to Nork, and before they grew close, they could hear the horrid squeaking of the rat-beasties and the Norkers shouting from outside. All three girls looked grim, and Restaria's face seemed pale. Deb petted Deecee's head for comfort, but even Deecee whined deep in his throat, sensing something terrible on the other side of the wall.

As they grew close to the wall, Stop and the men on top of it turned and saw her. They reacted with relief but also panic.

Stop, looking like he was about to cry yelled down, "Your Mayrshp, it's a terrible army! We are doomed!"

Restaria didn't answer. She simply climbed to the top of the wall. Deb climbed up as well, but Super, with her bad leg, stayed below with Deecee.

The women gazed out at the sea of gray monsters with their strange riders. It was a horrible sight, like something out of a nightmare. Because there was only the highway and tall buildings on either side, the rat-beasties crowded together and seemed to be everywhere. They moved and twitched, standing on their hind legs and sniffing the air around them or turning this way and that. The men of Nork yanked on the reigns of the ropes around their noses to try to keep them under control.

In the front of the army standing next to his fallen Harley, Moxie stood, smoking a cigar, his tommy-gun resting on his hip, grinning as if he'd won the battle already. He saw Restaria and took his cigar out of his mouth. He pointed at her with it.

"You the boss of these clowns? They let a dame like you in charge? Oh yeah, I remember you from last time."

Restaria instantly frowned, irritated at his male chauvinism. She replied angrily, "I am the leader of Letfreedomring. I will appreciate you addressing me with some respect and politeness!"

Deb looked down at Super. "She even talks like Misterwizard!" Super smiled back and nodded.

Moxie looked like he didn't understand what she said either, but just stood his ground, scowling. "Nuts."

Restaria continued. "We have already told you we will not pay tribute to your king. Please return to him and tell him, if he would like to be our friends, we will be glad to establish a trade system where we can benefit from each other. But we do not respond to threats."

Moxie chuckled, his eyes twinkling. A rat-beastie behind him rose on its hind legs and squeaked, as if listening to the conversation. It pawed the air with its pink little paws.

"Yeah, I figured you was gonna say somethin' like that, 'cause you think we was bluffin.' Listen sweetheart, you don't seem to get da picture. Look behind me. Now ya see what's coming your way?"

Restaria looked past him at the sea of rat monsters and the men riding them, then back at Moxie.

"Pretty terrifyin,' ain't it?" Moxie grinned bigger. "We come all the way from Nork, and we didn't come on no social visit. So, to show we mean bizness, the amount is now half what you got. Bring it out here and lay it on the grass. We'll take it back and see if it makes the Boss happy. I really hope ya don't, 'cause I came all this way, I'd like to have a little skirmish, if ya know what I mean."

He glanced back at the army with meaning, then back. "These ratties are getting mighty hungry."

Deb turned to Restaria. "Can you give them what they want?"

"We have barely enough to live on as it is," Restaria said. "And to collect half of what we have will take time."

From down below, Super yelled up. "How do they even know what half is? Just give them something to make them leave!"

Restaria smiled at this, and so did Deb. "Super's pretty smart," Deb said. "Just bluff 'em, tell them you'll give them what they want, then take your time while you plan what to do next."

"You girls have a lot of wisdom," Restaria said, smiling. "We can try, but I don't think we can rely on the

Nork warlord having much patience.”

Restaria turned back to Moxie. “We will give you what you want, but it will take us time.”

Moxie snorted. “You's got 'till the yellow eye is in the middle of the sky, then we better see something, or…” He made a slicing motion with his finger across his neck. “Sayonara, sister. Savvy?”

CHAPTER 17

Johnny and Starbucks ran down the street past the broken buildings around them to reach the first intersection. They arrived to see a flurry of activity. People ran everywhere, yelling at each other, crying and looking scared.

Starbucks turned to Johnny. "It looks like they've seen them!"

Johnny nodded. "Let's go find Deb, Super and Deecee!"

Johnny and Starbucks took off down the street towards the direction of Bell House where they'd left the girls. People ran by them, some men but mostly women, carrying scrabblers in their arms or dragging children after them. They didn't seem to know where they were going, for some ran back the way the boys had come, and others were running alongside them. It looked like disorganized chaos, people simply not sure what to do or where to go, but frightened.

A man named Sidestreet in a tattered suit that looked like nothing more than rags, his black hair sticking up on his head and stubble all over his chin ran up to them, carrying a sharp stick. He waved it in the air as he spoke.

"You're Johnny Apocalypse and his sidekick! Do something! Save us!"

Johnny and Starbucks stopped to talk to him. "Where is everyone going?"

Sidestreet waved the stick in the air, as if it was a live snake in his hand. "There's an army of men riding monsters outside the wall about to get in! Restaria has run away and left us to die! Lightpole, is nowhere to be found, and the army is in chaos!" He took off running.

Johnny turned to Starbucks. "You don't really think Restaria deserted them, do you?"

"We better find the girls and Deecee, fast!"

They ran down the street, past the old cars, broken-down buildings and people running everywhere. Suddenly they heard the bell from Bell House pealing.

"What does that mean, Johnny?" Starbucks asked as they continued to run.

"It sounds like war!"

The people around them become even more

agitated, running and screaming. Johnny had a feeling it wouldn't be long before the city was going to become a very dangerous place.

They finally reached Bell House to find a group of men gathering out front.

Johnny, encouraged, said, "It looks like they're getting their men together to fight, after all."

They ran inside. Men and women huddled on the floor, looking up, as if they thought the ceiling was going to fall on them at any second. But they didn't see Deb, Super or Deecee.

Johnny and Starbucks made a quick circuit of the building then joined at the front again. "Where could they be?"

An old woman lying on a blanket looked up and raised a bony, wrinkled finger. She pointed towards the north.

"They went to the north wall. An army of monsters has come!"

"Of course!" Starbucks said. "They're with Restaria on the wall facing that army!"

"Let's get there, fast!" Johnny said. They turned and ran out.

Charlie, Ticktock, Lady Stabs and Monsta continued their journey northward. As they weaved among the broken-down rusted cars along the strip of gray flat concrete that had once been a highway, they passed empty, decaying buildings on either side. Occasionally there would be gaps where they could see stretches of open field or roads leading off to who knew where. Despite her fear and exhaustion, Lady Stabs couldn't help but enjoy all the strange new scenery, knowing she was seeing new lands where she'd never been before.

They had to move at a fairly slow pace, for Monsta walked beside them, and he grew more tired by the minute. Lady Stabs wondered what would happen if Monsta just couldn't go on anymore, if they would kill him. She wouldn't feel bad about it if it happened, for he was a brute and a killer, but the thought of being left with the strange captors didn't fill her with happiness either. Monsta was not her friend, in fact he was an enemy, but he at least represented something familiar to home. If he was suddenly gone, she would be really alone.

Her captor, Charlie, noticed her looking around at their surroundings. He turned his head back towards her and grinned. "Hey Sis. Even though you're kind of a kooky dame with the hair and all, you're still a hot tomatah. If you think you could fall for a dope like me, I can fix things with the Boss. You and me can be, like you, know, steady, and you can be my moll. I can show you all around Nork. You'd really like it, I bet."

The thought of spending any time with the greasy, creepy gangster filled Lady Stabs with loathing, but she was smart enough to see an opportunity when she saw one. She smiled at him with a thoughtful look and tried to sound innocent and clueless.

"Do you really think you could fix things with your boss? I wouldn't want you to get into any trouble."

Encouraged, Charlie grinned wider, showing missing teeth, and his eyes lit up with joy. "Don't you worry about that, sweet chickadee. I'm a big shot back on Nork, you'll see, a big wheel. I'll show you around town, and show you off. I'll buy you the best threads, and you'll look like a million bucks."

"That sounds nice," Lady Stabs said, hoping he couldn't see the look of disgust on her face. "So, you know, my friend Monsta, can you maybe make 'em go a little easier on him?" Lady Stabs knew that even though she hated Monsta, he was still her best chance of escaping. "It's not that I really care, it's just, he's a friend, you know?"

Charlie chuckled. "Sure. Who knows, if your friend plays his cards right, maybe the boss will let him join us.

He can be somebody's lackey or somethin.'"

Charlie turned to Ticktock. "Hey, Ticktock, we ain't gonna get nowhere at this pace. That's guy's about had it. How about letting him ride Moxie's ratty for a while, just so he don't die?"

Ticktock frowned, suspecting a trap, and looked back at Monsta. Monsta was barely moving, his head down. Ticktock smiled, showing big white teeth. "All right. But he do something to Moxie's ratty, you're gonna take the rap."

"Sure, sure!" Charlie said, smiling at Lady Stabs with victory. She smiled back with gratitude.

Charlie turned to Monsta. "Hey dummy. Hey you!"

Monsta stopped and raised his head, looking like it weighed a ton. He stared at Charlie with weary eyes.

"Climb on that ratty in back. But don't try anything stupid, or we'll drill ya, got it?"

Monsta nodded with gratitude. He shuffled over to Moxie's ratty and struggled to get on.

"You better help him, Charlie, or we're gonna be here all night," Ticktock said.

Charlie groused, but then he climbed off and walked over to help Monsta on. He handed Monsta the reigns. "Now hold on and don't fall off. I ain't comin' to put ya on again."

Charlie walked back over and climbed back on his

ratty. He smiled once more at Lady Stabs. "See? I can be real friendly."

"Thank you," Lady Stabs said. "I'll remember that."

They kept riding for what seemed like hours, and Lady Stabs started to drift off. As they approached the city of Nork, Monsta had to fight off the desire to sleep too, having walked for miles. Lady Stabs lay with her head on Charlie's back, not moving, too tied to remember her revulsion at him or the rat-beastie.

They traveled down the remnants of a gray ribbon of road, with broken buildings on either side. Here, none of the buildings rose over one story and most were merely piles of rubble so they could see to the horizon in either direction. It was night, and all around them the buildings stretched on, mounded black shapes in the darkness. The destruction and emptiness weighed on Lady Stab's soul, and she felt sad. She began to wonder if this was all the world was now, a broken heap of yesterday, with no real chance to start again.

Beside them, Ticktock rode along, a smile on his face. He hummed to himself and glanced at Monsta once in a while, to make sure he wasn't trying anything.

Suddenly both men stopped their rattys. Monsta and Lady Stabs looked ahead. to see a giant wall surrounding the city. It rose up into the sky for what seemed like miles, and stretched as far as they could see in both directions. It was made of old cars, twisted steel and concrete and held together by heavy thick wire.

"Welcome to Nork, folks," Ticktock said. "Ain't you the lucky ones." He laughed in a dark way, and Charlie joined in. They started riding again.

Ticktock turned to Monsta. "Don't try nothing in there either, or you'll end up like one of them." He pointed at the wall. Monsta and Lady Stabs looked, and then they saw them. All over the wall, bodies hung, some just skeletons, others still covered with flesh and clothing. Was it just her imagination, or were some of the bodies still moving?

Lady Stabs gasped in horror. Ticktock laughed at her reaction. "That's what the Boss does with people he don't like."

"Yeah, you better hope he likes you, Monsta" Charlie said, chuckling darkly. "Or even me putting in a nice word for her ain't gonna matter."

Lady Stabs looked beyond the wall to see tall buildings like gray ghosts, as tall as the sky, raising up into the clouds, so many they seemed to stretch on forever. And on the tops of the buildings, she saw what she had seen so far away that filled her with dread. The tops of the buildings had what looked like the webs of spider-beasties draped all over them, from one building to another. Almost the top of every building was covered with them. The sight sent a chill running up and down her spine and she knew somehow it meant something terrifying lived there. She was about to ask Charlie about it, when Ticktock barked in a deep, commanding voice.

"Move! I want to get you mugs stowed so I can back to the fight before it's all over. Now!"

The rat-beasties started forward again, and Monsta shuffled on painfully. They headed towards the giant wall, and the city of Nork.

CHAPTER 18

estaria turned to Deb and Super. "We have to find a way to distract them while the people escape. I just don't know where we can go."

"You can go to New Sanctuary," Deb said, smiling. "Misterwizard and the people there will welcome you."

"I don't want to abandon our city, just when we were starting to build a home here, but we may have no choice," Restaria said.

Deb sighed. "I wish Johnny were here. He'd help you organize."

"Somebody call my name?"

The ladies all turned and looked down to see Johnny and Starbucks grinning up at them. Deecee barked and Johnny bent down as Deecee leapt into his arms, knocking him over and licking him.

"Easy, boy," Johnny said, laughing, and all the

other laughed with him.

"Johnny!" Deb said with joy, as she leapt into his arms just as he managed to stand up. Johnny grabbed her and kissed her. Starbucks walked over and petted Deecee, who waved his tail and licked his hand. Super, just as excited, decided to play it cool. She sauntered down the ramp nonchalantly as Starbucks watched her smiling.

When Super got close to Starbucks she said in a bored voice, "Miss me?"

"Like a mushroom monster," Starbucks said. They both laughed and then Super jumped into his arms and they kissed.

Starbucks looked down at her leg. "How's it?"

"Better," Super said, looking down at her leg too. "A little sore, but I can almost keep up with you again."

"You better," Starbucks said, and they kissed again, longer this time.

Restaria, pleased to see them but still with a look of worry on her face, walked down the ramp to join them.

"Johnny, I can't tell you how glad I am to see you and your friend."

Johnny still holding a smiling Deb around the waist, frowned in deep thought. "Starbucks and me saw the Nork army heading here and came back. We heard the loud thing in Bell House making noise. It looks like your men are gathering there."

Restaria nodded. "Yes, Lightpole is surely trying to organize them. I need to go there and help him."

"Hurry!" Deb said. "We don't have much time!"

Her words energized them all and together they turned and hurried back towards Bell House.

When they reached it, they found a scene of utter confusion. People ran back and forth through the dark, some carrying belongings, others dragging along scramblers by the hand. A large group of men stood in the square just in front of the building, arguing and yelling, a disorganized mob. In front of them stood a man with a bald head ringed by black hair, a pointed black mustache, and a pointed black beard. He yelled at the people, gesturing with an old sword he held in his hand.

Restaria and the rest ran up.

"Lightpole, I am here!"

The men all turned towards her with looks of relief, having finally someone to tell them what to do. The women running back and forth stopped and turned to look at her as well. Everyone gathered around in front of her, waiting to hear what she would say.

"Restaria, we are under attack!"

"Restaria, what do we do"

"Restaria, my children are terrified!"

"Restaria, help us!"

Restaria raised a reassuring hand and smiled at them, trying to allay their fears. Lightpole looked relieved to see her as well, though he wore a dark haughty look as if he was trying to show he wasn't afraid. He walked up to Restaria.

As he arrived, Johnny and his friends saw that he was of Asian descent. He wore a strange set of armor with metal plates and a black skirt. And he held a thin, long sword in his hand.

"Restaria, is it true we are under attack?" He asked her. "I've heard so many different stories!"

Restaria looked at him and nodded gravely. "The army from Nork has come to demand tribute. They are formidable, an army of men riding horrible rat-beasties."

Her words caused a ripple of fear to spread through the crowd and everyone whispered to each other at once.

Lightpole rose to attention and looked brave and fierce. "Command us, oh Restaria, and we will obey. The army stands ready to defend Letfreedomring!"

Restaria put a grateful hand on his shoulder and smiled at him. He continued to scowl with importance, but his pleasure at her touch shone in his eyes.

Restaria turned to address the crowd.

"We have to do two things in order to survive this

night. First, we need the women and children to gather as much supplies as they can to give to our attackers, in the hopes of appeasing them. I am not sure if this will work, and so the second thing must be readied as well. All the men must gather arms and prepare to defend the city while we find a way to bring our families someplace safe until we can find a way to fight them off."

Lightpole looked offended.

"You do not think that we can defeat them? We have been training and drilling for just this reason! My men are crack troops! We have developed weapons that will defeat any attackers at our walls!"

Another man piped up. "And now we have Johnny Apocalypse too!"

Restaria's eyes twinkled but she continued to look grim and shook her head.

"I know you are brave, and have prepared as best as you can. But when they came last time, they did not have the horrible rat-beasties with them and there were only a small band. Now they have a hundred or more and the monsters to ride and attack us. We did not prepare for such a large onslaught."

This caused another ripple to go through the crowd. Johnny stepped forward.

"Listen," Johnny said." They all looked at him and he continued. "I know you want to fight. You are just like my people when we fought and defeated the Gangers. At first, we had to run too, but once we grew organized, we beat them. It's not easy to run away, but sometimes it's the best plan, at least for a while."

Lightpole looked offended at the idea of running away, but the people all nodded and smiled. Johnny's words seemed to be coming from someone who knew what he was talking about, and it gave the people hope and allayed their fears a little.

Starbucks turned to Restaria. "Restaria, you should put as many of your army as you can on the walls, just in case the Nork army doesn't wait and attacks."

"Yes, that's a good idea. I think we should prepare everyone to leave and send only a small group with the offering. That will give the others time to escape."

Restaria turned to Johnny. "Johnny, I know you don't owe us anything, and you have just come to our city, but I feel as if you are truly our friends."

"We are!" Deb said.

Restaria turned and smiled at her, then turned back to Johnny. "Johnny, would you be willing to help Lightpole organize the army while I help the people escape? Your expertise in fighting will prove invaluable."

"Of course, Restaria. You just worry about the people. I'm sure Lightpole doesn't need my help, but I'll stay with him anyway."

"And Super and I will help you," Deb said.

"Let's get started," Restaria said. Turning to Deb and Super she said, "We don't have much time. Tell everyone you can find. Gather supplies and weapons, and gather all the children and weak ones at the south end of Pelpia. We must be ready to leave at a moment's notice!"

Johnny turned to Lightpole. "Lightpole, let's get your men up on the walls."

"Johnny Apocalypse!" Lightpole said in a regal voice. "It will be an honor to fight beside you. Together we will vanquish all our foes!"

Johnny grinned, liking Lightpole's bravado. "Do you have anything to fight with?

"Yes, we most certainly do!" Lightpole replied. "We may not have expected such a large army, but we're not as easily defeated as Restaria thinks. We'll show those ruffians a thing or two!"

"Great!" Johnny said, encouraged. He turned to Deb. "Deb, you take Deecee with you."

"Sure, Johnny!" Deb said.

Johnny, Starbucks and Lightpole took off in one direction with the men of the army towards the men of Nork as Restaria, Super, Deb and Deecee ran off in the opposite direction to gather the people.

A big, beefy man on a large rat-beastie rode up to Moxie. He wore different clothes, for instead of pants he wore what looked like a skirt with dark green and red squares on it. He held a big hatchet and across his white shirt he had a green sash. He also wore what looked like a flat mushroom shaped hat of green on his head.

Moxie stood next to his ratty smoking a big, smelly cigar.

"Tell me the truth, Moxie," the beefy man said. "Ayre we really gonna wait until the yellow eye be full to attack? My men ayre growing impatient for a wee bit of action. Ya didn't invite us all the way down here for a cup a tea, did ya?" The man's voice was gruff and he had a strange lilting accent.

"Okay, Clancy, it's time now," Moxie took a few more puffs, then grinned evilly and threw his cigar away. He picked up his Harley and sat on it, then raised his hand and shouted, "Let her rip, boys!"

Clancy grinned and rode his rat-beastie back to join his men.

Bugsy, Moxie's second in command grinned, raised his arm he yelled, "Attack!"

Behind Moxie a horrible shouting filled the air. The men on their rat-beasties started to move.

Like a horrible moving carpet, the rat-beasties ran towards the walls of Pelpia, silent and terrifying.

Suddenly they all grew excited and squeaked at once, filling the air with a horrible sound that made the skin crawl of even the men riding them.

Some of the rat-beasties got too excited and ran around in circles and just stood up, sniffing the air with their big, pointed noses. The men fought vainly to get them under control. One man fell off his rat-beastie and it scampered off. Before the man could get up, he was trampled by the rest of the rat-beastie army.

The rat-beasties reached the wall and seemed perplexed. They stopped and turned around, climbing all over each other.

Moxie watched from the very back of the army. "Get 'em to start climbing, you stupid lummoxes!" he yelled.

The men pulled on the reigns and pointed up the wall. The rat-beasties finally began to get the idea, and some tried to scale up, but the wall was tall. Still, the old metal cars and junk of the wall had lots of places for them to grasp with their paws, and some began to slowly ascend. Others climbed on the tops of the ones beneath them, making a rat-beastie ladder. The battle was on.

Meanwhile, Johnny, Lightpole and the men of Letfreedomring ran towards the wall. The men all looked fierce, shook their clubs and swords in the air and yelled war cries, but Johnny could tell they were scared inside.

He suspected none of them had actually fought a battle before, and he worried what would happen when they were tested.

They reached the wall, ran up and peered out into the darkness. With dismay, Johnny and the others realized they had just arrived in time. The rat-beasties came running towards the wall.

Lightpole jumped into action. "Men, you know what to do! It's up to us to defend our families. Deliver death to our enemies!"

He turned to Johnny with a grim smile. "We've been preparing for invaders for a while, though we hoped we'd never have to really face them. We have some tricks up our sleeve. Just watch!"

Johnny looked around, curious to see what Lightpole had planned.

CHAPTER 19

Restaria, Deb, Super and Deecee ran through the streets of Pelpia, stopping at every door to call inside.

Deb ran into an old building with only the bottom floor intact, her long blond hair flowing in the breeze from the dark, windy night. The walls of the upper floors were all broken and caved in, leaving the interiors exposed to the elements.

"Anyone here? Hello?"

A pair of old eyes peered at her from the darkness. An old man spoke, his voice seeming to float on the air. "What do you want? Who are you? You look like an angel."

Deb smiled slightly at the compliment, then spoke urgently. "You and your family have to join Restaria and us. There's an army attacking. We have to find a place to hide until it's safe!"

The voice of an older woman came floating out of the darkness. "We're too old to be running all over the city," she said. "Just leave us be. They won't hurt old people like us."

Deb thought about the army attacking. She knew the rat-beasties wouldn't care how old they were, they would attack and eat them anyway. She ran into the dark interior. She found an old couple lying on a mattress, curled up under one lone blanket. A pile of cans lay next to them, evidence of what they had to eat. A small candle, almost melted, stood on a wooden box. There was nothing else in the room except trash and debris.

Deb felt sorry for the old couple, and her heart hurt. She knelt down next to them. "Please. Let me help you. We'll find a way so you don't have to walk."

The old woman, her thin, white hair pasted on her forehead and the wrinkles in her face turning upwards into a smile, gazed at Deb with affection.

"You are a sweet young woman, Dearie. We don't have the strength left to go very far. You go save the younger people. Our lives are all used up."

Deb grew angry. "That's no way to talk. You're more valuable than anyone. You have the wisdom and knowledge the younger people need. I'm not leaving until you two get up and let me help you get to safety."

The old man and woman looked at each other with resignation. "I think she means it, Exit."

The old woman nodded. "I guess we'd better listen, Newsstand."

Slowly the old woman tried to rise. Deb smiled in victory and reached out to help her up. The old man raised himself on his elbow, and then with surprising energy sprung up to his feet. He took Exit's one elbow as Deb took the other. Together they led her towards the door.

"So, what is so urgent that you have to get an old, tired couple out of bed?" Newsstand said in a mildly grumpy voice.

"The army from Nork is attacking," Deb said. "An army of rat-beasties."

"Oh, dear," Exit said. "I hate rat-beasties. So dirty and horrible."

They reached the door to see the crowd let by Restaria already far down the street.

"Oh no!" Exit said in a shaky voice. "They're leaving you behind!"

"Leave us, before you put yourself in danger!" Newsstand said.

"I told you, you're coming with me," Deb said. "We'll catch up with them, don't you worry. I just have to find something for you two to ride on, that's all."

Deb had no idea where she was going to find something, but she knew she didn't have a lot of time before it was too late.

The Norkers grinned with dark pleasure as their rat-beasties rose higher and higher up the wall. In among the Norkers were other men on rat-beasties dressed much like Clancy, wearing the same strange skirts. Some held hatchets, others clubs.

Suddenly on top of the wall appeared men, lots of them. As the men of Nork watched with surprise, the men of Letfreedomring raised bows and pointed them towards the rat-beasties. As the men of Nork watched in dismay, the men fired arrows down on the invading army.

Rat-beasties were pierced with the arrows and reacted screeching and pawing at the arrows. Some fell back, dumping their men on the ground. Others ran off altogether, with their riders trying in vain to control them. Some bit at the arrows and tried to pull them out as their riders tried to help them.

But more rat-beasties piled in behind the ones who fell back. The men of Letfreedomring reloaded and shot again, and another wave of rat-beasties fell to the ground, shrieking in pain.

Johnny, Starbucks and Lightpole stood at the front of the defenders, each with swords in their hands to fight any rat-beasties that made it to the top.

More rat-beasties came, and now some climbed on the bodies of others that had fallen. Some were getting dangerously close to the top of the wall.

Lightpole yelled, "Bring the oil!"

Men ran up with buckets of oil. They ran to the edge and poured it over, onto the rat-beasties below. The rat-beasties, not liking the smell of feel of the oil, stopped climbing and sniffed at their bodies, unsure what to do.

"Burn them, men!" Lightpole yelled, his eyes lit with dark fire.

As the men of Nork watched with horror, torches were thrown over the side of the wall. It ignited the oil and soon the rat-beasties became living torches. They screeched in agony and ran away, or lay on the ground, writhing in pain. As they ran into other rat-beasties they caught their fur on fire as well. Soon living torches ran off into the darkness, with burning rat-beasties and men both screaming in their death throes. Chaos took over the Nork army and the push to attack began to falter.

Moxie, watching from his Harley, cursed and spat

on the ground.

Bugsy sitting on a rat-beastie next to him yelled down, "These mugs are tougher than they look, Moxie!"

"Tell the stupid idjits to stop trying to take 'em head-on, Lame-brain! Circle around the joint and look for a place where they ain't fighting back!"

Bugsy nodded. "Good thinkin,' Moxie!" He pulled on the reigns of his rat-beastie and rode off to give the order.

Restaria, Super, Deecee and the people of Letfreedomring hurried towards the south end of Pelpia. They ran down the main street, now a crowd so large that they filled it all the way to the buildings on either side. Some ran, others moved slowly, helping the elders or little children. All followed Restaria, who waved her arm in the air and kept shouting so they'd know where to go.

Super tried to keep up with her bad leg. She turned to Restaria as they hurried along. "Do you have a plan where to go?"

Restaria nodded. "If we have to, head towards Ballmor. At least it will give us a place to regroup."

"Uh," Super said, "Remember there are already monsters there, the Krakn. What about inland?"

"Inland is also dangerous," Restaria replied. "There are roving tribes that live there. Though they may be better to face than the monsters."

"Maybe just take them to Sanctuary," Super suggested."

"That's a long way!" Restaria replied. "You said it was on the other side of Balmor."

"No, I don't mean our new Sanctuary, I mean the old one. It had walls and a place to defend."

Restaria nodded, interested. "Didn't the Doomsday Prophecy destroy it?"

Super replied, "Probably, but it's a place to try, at least."

Restaria listened, interested.

Super continued. "It's across the rushing water, which will also be a good defense."

Restaria smiled at them. "You are very smart, and I appreciate all the help you're trying to give. If we need to, can you lead us to this old Sanctuary?"

"Of course!" Super said, smiling brightly "But you could always go to New Sanctuary too. If you only had some yellow buses."

"Yellow buses?" Restaria asked, her eyes laughing.

"Hey," Super started, then thought for a moment. "You don't have an underground, do you, like Washington Deecee?"

Restaria looked confused. "Underground? You mean the subway? It would be a trap, with no way out, and most of the entrances have been destroyed."

"How about going up?" Super said. "Up into the buildings?" Super pointed at the broken building around them and looked at them. They looked dark and foreboding in the night sky, like looming ghosts. "No, I guess that wouldn't work either," Super said.

"We'd be just as trapped there. No, we have to find a way to escape, at least find a place that will shelter us for a little while."

They reached the wall at the south end of Pelpia where Johnny and Starbucks and the girls had arrived what seemed like ages ago. Restaria sighed with relief and leaned on the wall, looking exhausted. Super, also tired from all the activity, sat on a broken piece of concrete and rubbed her leg.

The people soon joined them and created a huge crowd, milling about, talking excitedly and looking lost and confused.

"So, which is it going to be, Restaria?" Super asked as she leaned on the rusty orange hulk of an old car.

"For now," Restaria said wearily as she pushed herself away from the wall, "we will go towards this old Sanctuary of yours. With the river and its structures, it may provide us with a place to defend, for a small time."

Super nodded. "Sounds like the best plan you can make, for now."

Suddenly from outside the wall they heard a terrible screeching. Restaria and Super looked at each other in alarm. Quickly they climbed the ramp to the top of the wall and peered out in the darkness.

From far away in the shadows, monstrous creatures glided towards them, hundreds of them, dark shapes crawling along like giant spiders. Restaria turned to Super, her face drained of all color.

"Oh, oh," Super said. "Are those the Krakn from Balmor?"

"Yes," Restaria said with fright, nodding her head. "They're coming here to attack as well!"

CHAPTER 20

Charlie, Ticktock, Lady Stabs and Monsta reached the wall at the front of Nork. From windows inside the wall, two men, one on either side of a giant gate, peered down at them. They pointed the Tommy guns down at them, and Lady Stabs wondered if they were going to shoot them.

Ticktock waved up at them and the two men grinned and nodded. The giant gate, which seemed to be on some sort of metal rope, swung open with a loud ear-piercing screech. Every one of them winced, even Charlie and Ticktock, until the sound finally groaned to a stop.

They rode inside, into the Nork wonderland. Behind them, the gate ground closed again. Lady Stabs turned and watched it with foreboding, knowing she was trapped inside now. It wouldn't be easy to scale that wall. It seemed as high as the sky.

She sighed, wishing once again she'd never left

Sanctuary. As she gazed ahead, it seemed to Lady Stabs as if the tall structures went on forever, the street stretching to the horizon with nothing but buildings as far as the eye could see. The yellow eye was just peeking over the buildings on the horizon, its light shining between them, giving the ones in front a black silhouette that made them look sinister. The buildings looked like tall, old guards to Lady Stabs, sleeping, just waiting for someone to make a noise so they would awaken and turn and attack.

They rode down an empty street, but Lady Stabs was surprised to see few old rusted cars. Even though the street and buildings had the same green, moldy look of age, they seemed free of trash and junk, as if someone had done some work cleaning up. There were metal barrels in the streets, and they had fires in them. And gathered around all of them were people! They looked like wildies, warming themselves by the fire, men, women and scrabblers. They shuffled about and wandered around, and there seemed to be a lot of them. From somewhere, she heard music. It sounded like some sort of instrument, and it was pleasant and somehow strangely comforting.

The people were dirty and wore ragged clothes. They looked hungry and tired. Some were old, others were of all ages, some just scrabblers holding onto the hem of their mothers' ragged dresses or chasing each other and playing games.

Then she saw men dressed like Charlie and Ticktock walking around amongst the people. There were only a few of them, but they carried guns and wore suits with stripes just like all the men did. They were obviously better fed and clothed than the ordinary people, and the people around them watched them with fear and respect. They were the men in charge, Lady Stabs figured, the Boss's soldiers.

Lady Stabs looked back at Charlie and Ticktock and noticed they kept looking up at the tops of the buildings, as if wary of something. She'd noticed the guards and the people seemed to be constantly scanning the skies as well. She turned her gaze up to the tops of the buildings too and saw what she had seen from a distance before. The tops of the buildings did have spider-beastie webs!

All the buildings had some sort of webs spanning the distance between them, all at the very top. They made a whole network of webs all around the city. The thought of what horrible creature made those webs made her shudder and she looked down, hoping she'd never have to find out what made them.

Lady Stabs looked back at Monsta. He was awake now too, gazing around, taking in the sights just like her, but she was sure he was planning on how to do some kind of mischief. She saw him look up at the webs too, and wondered what he thought about them.

She looked at Charlie. He wore a smile as he looked around, and she could tell it was because he was back at his home where he was happy.

"This is it, Honey," he said with a grin. "Nork. You're gonna really like it here. A dame with moxie can really make it in this town, go places. If they got a guy like me to open doors for 'em."

Lady Stabs nodded at him smiling, wishing he would suddenly drop dead.

Ticktock pulled on the reigns of his rat-beastie and it slowed down. He waited until Monsta was next to him.

"Hey, dude," Ticktock said to Monsta. Monsta seemed to be lost in looking around and kept going. Ticktock reached over with his leg and kicked Monsta with his foot. Monsta finally stopped and turned towards him.

"Time for you to get off Moxie's ratty again. You can walk the rest of the way."

Monsta scowled, and he just sat there, challenging him. Ticktock's jaw tightened and his eyes looked dangerous. Monsta backed down, and slowly climbed off the rat-beastie.

Ticktock looked satisfied and grabbed the reigns

of Moxie's rat-beastie. He pulled it back and tied the reigns to his saddle.

"Just wait until you meet, the Boss," Charlie said to Lady Stabs, looking over his shoulder and grinning at her. "They don't call him the King of Nork for nothin.' He's gonna be the king of the world someday. We're gonna take it all over, and then I'm gonna be in charge of my own whole city, maybe a whole bunch of 'em!"

Lady Stabs just smiled back cheerily. What she was really thinking about was where and when to make a break for it.

"You can be my moll when that happens," Charlie said. "I'll make sure you got the fanciest rags and all the ice you can wear. You'll be the cat's meow then."

"Uh-huh," Lady Stabs said, finding Charlie, ugly, annoying and irritating but trying not to show it. He didn't smell as if he understood what washing was either, and she had been struggling not to retch as she held onto him during their ride. The thought of him touching her, let alone kissing her gave her the creeps, but she had to play along.

"Tell me, Charlie," she said in an off-hand, casual way, "what's up above us?"

Charlie turned to look at her, and his serious expression surprised her. "Just keep an eye peeled for them buildings. When they attack, it's all sudden-like.

And you better hope they don't have the buggys with 'em."

"Stinkin' Angels," Ticktock said, eyeing the buildings above them eyes filled with anger. "The Boss'll take care of 'em someday soon, for good."

The angels, Lady Stab thought. Her curiosity doubled, and so did her apprehension. When they attacked?

She fell silent, thinking, as they padded along. They came to a road that seemed empty and quiet. Charlie seemed edgy, glancing around everywhere. Even Ticktock gazed around as if expecting an attack any minute.

Montsa, a little more rested after riding the rat-beastie, smiled in a friendly way and struck up a conversation. "Hey, Ticktock, we got off to a bad start. You know, I really like you guys. Maybe I could join your group, you know? I used to be a member of a gang called the Doomsday Prophecy. And I got some stuff I could tell your boss that he might find pretty interestin.'"

Ticktock snorted. "'Zat so?"

Lady Stabs scowled and glared at Monsta. Here he was, ready to sell out Johnny and his tribe again. He was just like Ripper, a snake and a louse. She wished she could take Ticktock's gun and shoot him, but she knew that wasn't going to happen. She gritted her teeth and wished again she could find a way to escape.

"Information, what kind of information?" Charlie said.

"He's talking to me, Stupid," Ticktock said.

Charlie scowled and looked forward again, knowing Ticktock was no one to mess with.

"What you got?" Ticktock said. "If it seems worth somethin,' maybe we'll talk."

"Hey!" Lady Stabs suddenly said, trying to distract them and cut Monsta off. "Look over there!" She pointed to a side street.

They all looked, but there was nothing there.

"I don't see nothin,'" Charlie said.

Suddenly from above them fireballs fell, striking the ground all around them. The rat-beasties shrieked and rose up on their hind legs. More fireballs fell. The people around them began to scream and run for cover.

Lady Stabs looked up, and saw the most terrifying thing she'd seen yet. Her mind went blank with fear and amazement. As she watched, a giant spider-beastie climbed down the side of the building towards them!

She screamed and grabbed Charlie's shoulders in a vise grip. On the ground, the people scattered, screaming in terror.

More fireballs hit the ground, making small fires spring up.

"The Angels are attacking!" Ticktock yelled savagely, and he pulled out his gun and started shooting it wildly. The rat-tat-tat sound filled the air and hurt Lady Stabs' ears. Suddenly she felt like she was underwater, the whole world becoming some kind of dream.

Charlie and Lady Stabs fell off the rat-beastie which scampered off. Ticktock untied Moxie's rat-beastie and it took off too. Monsta ran away as Ticktock fought to get his rat-beastie under control.

The giant spider stopped on the side of a building.

Charlie scampered up and grabbed his rifle. He swung it around, looking for something to shoot. "Hurry! Get to cover!"

As Lady Stabs struggled to get up, she saw something amazing. Long, slim figures in white swung down on ropes from the buildings above them. They were men and women, all tall and thin, with slight bodies and long white hair. They all reminded her Deb, for their hair was just like hers. The men and women held bows and arrows. They landed on the ground and aimed their bows. As she watched, they shot some of the closer guards, who fell with arrows sticking out of them. They seemed to be ignoring the ordinary people and just concentrating on the guards. Then they turned towards Charlie, Ticktock and Lady Stabs.

Charlie turned his gun to shoot at one of them,

but before he could, an arrow struck him in the throat. He grabbed at it as Lady Stabs screamed.

Three arrows struck Ticktock's rat-beastie. It screeched and fell over, twitching. Ticktock jumped off and ran away, disappearing into a building.

Lady Stabs finally stood up as the white men and women approached her, bows drawn. She put her hands up and tried to look harmless.

The men and women wore little clothing, just filmy robes tied with golden belts at the waist with no arms and small white shoes that looked like some kind of soft fabric. They gazed at her with dark menace that showed no fear, their bows and arrows pointed at her.

"Please! I'm not with them! I'm a stranger! I was their prisoner!"

A beautiful woman with long, blond hair, a long face with a long nose and dark, sultry eyes spoke in a confident, haughty voice.

"You are not a friend of the Norkers?"

Lady Stabs, her mind numb, shook her head. "No! I'm from a tribe a long-ways away from here. I was captured. Please don't kill me."

The woman turned to the others and whispered. Lady Stabs could hear them talking intently, the only word she understood was "friend."

The woman motioned with her bow towards the

building. "Come with me. Or die. Your choice."

Lady Stabs quickly walked the way the woman indicated, not being able to take her eyes off the giant spider-beastie that just sat there, its furry arms twitching.

One of the men waved his hand towards the sky. As she watched with amazement, a huge basket was lowered down from the top of the building with four ropes.

The men and women picked up Charlie's dead body and dumped it in the basket. She wondered what they wanted with it; were they some sort of sick cannibals who eat people?

The group led Lady Stabs over to the basket and the woman motioned for her to get in. Lady Stabs wondered what strange and bizarre adventure she'd stumbled into now. With trepidation, she climbed into the basket, trying to stay as far away from Charlie's body as she could.

With surprise she saw the men and women didn't join her, but grabbed onto the ropes they had descended on. In a flash they rose up into the air, holding on with only one hand.

She shrieked as the basket began to rise. He peered over and saw the spider-beastie crawling back up the building. She was being lifted up towards the sky. Just where were they taking her?

CHAPTER 21

Johnny, Starbucks and Lightpole ran along the top of the wall, their eyes looking outside of the city. There in the darkness next to the wall they saw dark, gray shapes scurrying along, with darker shapes sitting on them. The Nork army was looking for a way in.

"Johnny!" Starbucks yelled, remembering something. "The hole in the wall we went through!"

Johnny stopped and turned to look at Starbucks grimly. Lightpole stopped too and looked from one to the other.

Johnny turned to Lightpole. "Lightpole, there's an opening in the wall. It's how we got in. If the Nork army gets there before we do…"

"We must hurry!" Lightpole said, his face grave.

They ran along the wall again, this time with extra urgency.

When they reached the spot where the opening was, they were relieved to see the Norkers hadn't reached it yet. But in the distance further up the wall they could hear the awful squeaking.

"How can we fix it?" Lightpole said, his body trembling with excitement and tension.

"Do we have time?" Starbucks said, the yellow eye glinting off his dark skin.

Suddenly another soldier from Letfreedomring ran up to the wall on the inside, his face full of terror and hopelessness. He was a young man, tall and thin like a bunch of beanpoles tied together. His eyes shone white with fear in the darkness. He ran up to wall, looked at Lightpole and waved his arms in the air frantically.

"They've climbed over the north wall! There was nothing we could do! We fought as long as we could! We had to run!"

Lightpole slumped, looking defeated. He spoke in a grim but courageous voice. "Then it doesn't matter about this hole. They'll be coming fast. We have to hold them until our people have a chance to escape."

He turned to the thin young man. "Firstclassmail, run on to the south wall and tell Restaria! She needs to know!"

Firstclassmail nodded, his face a mask of fear. He turned and ran on as fast as he could, disappearing again into the darkness.

Johnny, Starbucks and Lightpole climbed down the wall back into Pelpia again.

Suddenly another man came running from the opposite direction, this one short and fat, huffing and puffing out of breath. He ran so hard he ran into Lightpole, knocking them both down.

"Look where you're going Tunasandwich!" Lightpole said grumpily, as he sat up and dusted himself off.

"I-I'm sorry, Lord Lightpole," Tunasandwich stammered out. "B-But I have some terrible news."

As Lightpole struggled up, Tunasandwich just sat on the ground trying to catch his breath.

"Well, give it to us then," Lightpole said, as he straightened the metal plates of his armor. "No good news today. We haven't got any of that for a long time."

Tunasandwich shook his head back and forth and seemed on the verge of tears. "Monsters are attacking to the south! Weird creatures with long arms and legs! They are hideous and frightening!"

"To the skies above!" Lightpole screamed. "Do the mushroom monsters hate us so much they've decided to finish us off? Have we offended them somehow more than all the other rabble in this world?"

Johnny and Starbucks gazed at each other.

"The Krakn," Johnny said.

"It sure seems like everything's coming against them at once," Starbucks said.

Johnny put his hand on his chin, deep in thought.

"But maybe this is the best thing to happen."

"What are you talking about?" Lightpole asked curiously, hoping for any glimmer of good news.

Johnny grinned, looking devilish in the dark. "If we could arrange for the Norkers and the Krakn to meet..."

Starbucks grinned, catching on. "They can finish each other off!!"

"Quick!" Johnny said. "If we get on our Harleys, maybe we can get the Krakn's attention. Then we can lead them right into the Nork army!"

"It's going to be dangerous and probably suicidal, so let's do it!" Starbucks said, grinning with glee.

"Lightpole," Johnny said, "You just keep the Norkers distracted long enough for me and Starbucks to get to the south gate. Then we'll see if we can't give the Norkers something else to worry about."

Lightpole smiled with a glimmer of hope. Tunasandwich smiled too, staring at them with his hand supporting himself behind his body, sitting on his rump.

"Good luck, Johnny. Take care!"

Johnny and Starbucks climbed down the wall and

out the hole to their Harleys. Starting them up, the roared off into the darkness.

Restaria and Super watched with horror as the Krakn advanced on the wall of Pelpia. More and more poured out from the darkness, crawling along on their four legs, their four arms holding clubs or sticks and just waving in the night air.

"Is this world filled with monsters now?" Restaria asked. "I thought the rat-beasties were bad enough, but these things are even worse! What are we going to do?"

Super wished she had an answer, but panic and desperation seeped into her mind as well. They couldn't go north, for they'd run right into the teeth and paws of the rat-beasties and the swords of the Nork army. They couldn't go south, because a terrible army of monsters was waiting to eat them. They were trapped. Super didn't see any way out.

Super gazed at the people gathering in the streets inside the wall. They filled the street as far as she could see and some waited inside the brick buildings on either side of the street, hiding there and peering out. There were so many of them, and they looked lost, worried.

Little scrabblers held onto their mothers and gazed around with scared looks. The mothers and fathers looked scared as well, wanting to go somewhere, to do something to escape. Most of them looked up to Restaria, waiting for her to tell them what to do.

None of them had weapons. Super was about to suggest to Restaria that they all just hide in the buildings when she heard a familiar and welcome bark. Despite the danger she grinned down, happy to see Deecee below staring up at her. Next to him stood Deb, Newsstand and Exit.

"Sorry we're late," Deb said. "We're a little slower than most. So, what's the plan?"

Far away, but too close, from the darkness to the north came a horrible squeaking. The Nork army was almost on top of them too!

"We have to get the people out of here!" Super yelled.

Deb looked with dismay at the older couple as Restaria and Super ran past her to the people of Letfreedomring. Deb helped the older couple and they turned and followed as fast as they could.

Restaria reached the crowd and they all turned towards her. She breathed in deeply and braced herself, a look of sorrow on her face.

"Listen to me, people of Letfreedomring. We

have no choice but to go inside these buildings around us and barricade ourselves in until the army has a chance to fight our enemies. Go up as high as you can and try to block the doors."

A woman with a look of terror and clutching her little girl scrabbler screamed, "Why can't we leave the city? The Nork army is coming right now!"

Super stepped forward to answer her. "Because there are other monsters coming from the south too, just as bad."

"She's led us into a trap!" A short, fat man in a pair of shorts and a ragged tee shirt wailed, his black curly hair sticking straight up on his head.

"She can't help it if the city is being attacked!" Super said.

Restaria put a hand on Super's shoulder and smiled at her. Then she looked at the crowd. "People of Letfreedomring. It seems we have no choice but to take shelter for the moment. But do not despair. Our army is fighting for us, and we will find a way to win, I promise you!"

The crowd murmured grumpily, seeming unconvinced.

Super put her hands on her hips and yelled angrily, "You need to listen to Restaria now, and hurry, before it's too late, or there won't be any of you left to save!"

The people all began talking and shouting at once, but then they finally began breaking off into groups, heading towards the nearby buildings.

"Please, don't panic!" Restaria said, afraid they might trample each other in their haste. "We still have time. Take care of each other!"

Most of the people didn't hear her though, they were too busy trying to get to the buildings ahead of anyone else. Soon they disappeared into the dark interiors of the buildings.

Restaria moved to help them find places. Super walked off in a different direction to help people find places as well.

Deb looked at Newsstand and Exit. "Come on! We have to find a place for you to hide!"

Newsstand smiled sadly. "Let the young people protect themselves. There's not enough room for old people like us." Exit nodded in agreement.

"Don't be silly," Deb said, worried. "The younger people need their elders to teach them and guide them. You're the most important ones of all. Now come along, or I'll drag you!"

Reluctantly, Newsstand and Exit let Deb push them towards the nearest building, a four-story brick one with a ragged green awning. The large front window, half-shattered, still had the letters, "Barb" on them, and on the side of the door was a strange little pole with red, white and blue stripes on it.

Deb led Newsstand and Exit inside. Then she saw something. Deecee was by himself, wandering around sniffing at the overgrown grass and old metal poles near the street. "Looking for Johnny, Deecee?" Deb said, smiling. "I miss him too. Come here, before the monsters get here. Deecee!"

Deecee didn't listen, instead he began trotting away, in the direction of the Nork army!

Deb scowled, and fear gripped her for a second as she ran after Deecee. The last thing she wanted to see was him getting eaten by one of the rat-beasties.

To her dismay, Deecee, who acted like he thought nothing at all was wrong, trotted down the street, getting further away.

"Deecee! You come back! Deecee!"

Deb noticed most of the people had made it inside the buildings. She could see some in the dark interiors, dark shadows passing by the windowless openings of the buildings. Some had lit torches, and the cheery orange light bobbed as they walked around inside.

A chill ran through Deb and she hugged herself. It was a cold night, and despite her leather jacket and jeans, she felt cold. Her long blond hair floated in a breeze and she wished she had Johnny there to hold her and keep her warm.

And comfort her. She suddenly felt so alone and missed Johnny, seeing his warm, confident smile that always made her feel safe and like he always knew just what to do next.

A slight feeling of panic gripped her as she hurried after Deecee. If anything happened to him, Johnny would never forgive her. Why did the dumb dog-beastie have to take now to go on an exploring trip? She hurried through the darkness, searching for him. "Deecee! Come back!"

CHAPTER 22

Moxie watched with glee as the rattys finally reached the top of the wall and climbed over. The men of Pelpia shot arrows and fought with swords, but now the rattys were on them. The Nork men jumped off their mounts once they reached the top of the wall and fought. Then the rattys bit the Norkers and the Clansmen too, apparently not trained to only eat enemies. Moxie scoffed. The men of Pelpia were weak and spineless. As soon as the rattys reached the top, they ran away, screaming like little scrabblers.

Moxie laughed as he watched a ratty grab a man from Pelpia in its mouth and bite him. The man screamed in pain and squirmed as the ratty swung him through the air. After a few moments, the man went quiet. The ratty dropped him on the top of the wall and started eating him.

Moxie turned his eyes away from the pleasant sight and turned his attention to the gate. He climbed on his new toy and started it up, hearing the roar as its engine came to life. He was really beginning to like this new thing. He turned the handle like Monsta taught him, and this time he rode away slow and smooth. He was getting the hang of it!

He rode towards the gate, a big grin on his face, feeling like a king on his mighty steed. He reached the gate too fast and realized he didn't remember how to stop the thing! He figured it out at the last minute, but not before he crashed into the gate and fell over again.

Angry at the pain in his leg and how stupid he looked, he banged on the gate with his hand.

"Hey! Lamebrains! Open the gate, ya dumb palookas! Hurry up!"

He forgot all about the pain and his fall when the gate creaked open. He smiled with dark delight. They were inside. The killing and fun were just beginning.

Inside Pelpia, the nightmare was just starting. The men of Pelpia ran, not even trying to fight back, as the rat-beasties with their men on their backs chased them. As Moxie picked up his Harley again and got ready to ride inside, he thought how this was no real battle, it was just a plain old-fashioned whooping. How he loved to see good old-fashioned death and destruction!

In a way, he was glad to be here, far away from home, where he was in charge, not the Boss. He was king out here, and he didn't have to deal with all the problems back home that made living there such a constant irritation. Here he could do what he wanted and there was no one to tell him different. And he didn't have to worry about being dragged off by an angel.

It occurred to him that the Boss might not want them totally destroying the Pelpia dudes, he might want them left alive to pay tribute and stuff. But he thought to himself, if that didn't happen, well, he could just tell the Boss they gave him and the guys no choice, they had to kill 'em or be killed themselves. *Yeah, that would work,* he thought.

As he started his Harley and slowly drove into the city, he felt like a conqueror riding into a defeated foe's city. It made him feel warm and happy inside. Then he thought, *Wait a minute, Moxie; if you don't kill 'em all, maybe you can be the Boss's boss here in this town, run things.* Yeah, he liked that idea. He decided he'd better catch up to the guys to tell 'em to take it easy. He didn't want them killing everybody and souring the deal.

He gave the Harley gas and sped off, as more rattys and Nork riders poured in the gate behind him.

Johnny and Starbucks rode through the darkness, weaving down the street that ran next to the wall. In the dark, the old rusted cars and piles of trash looked like black, indistinguishable shapes, and they constantly had to slow down and maneuver around them. It took time, and Johnny began to feel panic setting in. They didn't have time to waste!

Starbucks looked up at the wall then pointed at it. "Johnny, look!"

Johnny looked and saw what Starbucks was pointing at. There was a whole section of wall that had collapsed inward, leaving a hole big enough to ride a bus through.

Johnny grinned at Starbucks. "I guess it didn't matter about the hole after all." Starbucks grinned back. They turned and continued fighting their way around all the junk in the street.

Suddenly in front of them they heard an all-too familiar horrible screeching. They looked at each other and nodded. The Krakn were just ahead.

"What's our plan, Johnny?" Starbucks yelled over the roar of his engine.

"We'll let 'em see us, make noise with our

engines. If that don't work, we'll have to find a way to make 'em more interested in us than the wall."

Starbuck's eyes, white in the darkness, showed uneasiness, "I don't like the sound of that."

"Neither do I," Johnny yelled.

The screeching grew louder. Soon they could see dark, horrible shapes with lots of arms and legs crawling through the darkness. Johnny's skin crawled, and his common sense spoke to him, "What are you doing? Once they see you, you're dead!"

Johnny forced himself to ignore the thoughts, even though they were perfectly reasonable questions to ask, and tried to concentrate on his plan of action.

Johnny glanced over at Starbucks, who seemed to blend into the night and was hard to see because of his dark skin color. All Johnny could see was Starbuck's white eyes staring forward, looking scared. It made Johnny grin, knowing he wasn't the only one a little frightened at the moment.

"Starbucks, let's stop when we get close and roar our engines."

Starbucks turned to look at Johnny and grinned, and now Johnny could see his bright white teeth.

"You got it!"

Despite the danger, Jonny grinned in the darkness. If he had to face danger, he couldn't think of anyone he loved having by his side more than his best friend Starbucks. Somehow it made him less scared and even made the danger seem fun.

They drove slower, their engines making puttering sounds as they glided down the highway. Ahead of them they saw what looked like hundreds of dark shapes flitting around old cars, over piles of trash and hanging to the sides of buildings. It was like a scene from a nightmare.

Johnny tried to quiet his beating heart. Despite having faced danger before, he still found fear crawling up his insides. He remembered how fast these creatures were, and thought about all the junk in the streets. Once they were spotted, if they got stuck anywhere, they'd be doomed.

"Okay, Starbucks," Johnny said, his voice sounding much shakier than he wanted it to. "Let's do it here!"

Johnny and Starbucks could see the south wall of Pelpia to their left disappearing into the darkness. The Krakn swarmed at the bottom of it like a bunch of spider-beasties, crawling over each other, trying to climb up. Johnny knew they didn't have much time.

"Here goes!" Johnny revved his engine, and a second later Starbucks did too. The sound filled the night air with sound. It made Johnny's heart skip a beat with fear, and as he looked at Starbucks, he noticed that he too looked scared.

They watched the Krakn, tense as bowstrings, ready to turn and take off at any second. A few Krakn who had been rushing towards the wall stopped and looked at them, their ragged black mouths opening and their black eyes searching the darkness for the sound.

"They see us, Johnny" Starbucks whispered.

"Not enough," Johnny said. They needed to get the whole horde's attention. Johnny gritted his teeth.

"Turn around, Starbucks, and get ready to ride fast. I'm going to get their attention!"

As Starbucks watched, Johnny hunkered down and took off with a roar. Starbucks worked on turning his Harley around. Then he watched over his shoulder, his hand on the throttle, ready to move.

Johnny rode fast and pulled his sword out of its sheath on his belt. Holding it high, he picked one of the Krakn and rode right for it.

The Krakn was a big one who towered above Johnny. Johnny's mind went blank as he concentrated on what he was doing. He drove right up to the Krakn. It turned at the last minute and saw him. It screeched.

Johnny swerved his Harley and spun the tire so he was right next to it. Then he swung his sword and cut off one of the Krakn's legs. It screeched in pain and reared back.

Johnny roared his engine. "Hey! Over here, you ugly monsters! Come eat me if you can! "

His actions had the desired effect. All the Krakn piling up at the wall stopped and turned their heads then their body and stared at him. They saw a lone, dark figure on some strange device with the light of one headlight stabbing into the darkness.

A loud screech filled the air. Johnny looked and saw the leader of the Krakn at the back of the horde. It stared directly at him. Then it pointed with one of its tentacles.

Before Johnny could react, the whole horde turned and scampered towards him. They definitely were single minded, and could be distracted towards any movement. In a panic, Johnny clumsily turned his Harley around.

Remembering something Misterwizard once said in a similar situation he yelled, "Damn the torpedoes! Full speed ahead!" though he had no idea what it meant. He gunned his engine and took off, just in time. The first Krakn were almost on top of him!

He sped off into the darkness, his heart in his throat, hoping desperately he didn't get blocked by an old car or a pile of trash and have to stop. He sped down the dark street, barely able to see where he was going.

His tires spun on the slimy vegetation covering the street. Darker shapes in the dark night loomed everywhere in front of him.

His engine sputtered, and for a moment Johnny was terrified that it was going to quit, but then it caught again. A Krakn ran up right next to him, its horrid mouth open and its sharp teeth chattering. It reached out from him with one of its tentacles.

Johnny slashed at it desperately, and it pulled the tentacle back, but now another on the other side ran up. Johnny tried to give the engine more gas, feeling as if at any moment they were going to grab him and yank him off the Harley.

A giant pile of trash, old metal and wood, stood right in Johnny's path. He couldn't turn either way, for the Krakn were right next to him on either side. He gritted his teeth and pulled back on the handlebars.

Johnny's Harley sped up the trash pile. The Krakn on either side of him screeched and ran around the pile on either side. Johnny rose up, higher and higher until he reached the top. Then he was soaring through the air, hoping desperately he would land on the ground without crashing.

The ground rose up to meet him, and Johnny braced himself for impact. Suddenly one of the Krakn was right below him! He landed on its back with a soft thud, and it squashed down, its four tentacle legs and four arms splayed out like a squashed bug-beastie.

Johnny fell sideways and the Harley skittered away. He jumped up and ran to get back on it fast. The Krakn came after him. He was sure he wasn't going to make it!

Suddenly Starbucks rode up, sword in hand.

"Hey ugly! Over here!"

Starbucks slashed at the Krakn about to bear down on Johnny, cutting one of its legs. It stopped and screeched then took off after Starbucks.

Johnny, his heart full of gratitude and relief, picked up his Harley, started it and took off again. He sped off down the street between two rusted cars, one lying on its back with the doors open. He sighed an immense sigh of relief. But then he worried whether the Krakn were still following him. He glanced back.

Oh yes, they were, he realized. He could see their dark shapes crawling over old cars and buses, crawling along the sides of buildings and bounding down the street. The added activity of fighting the two Krakn had made them even more agitated.

He suddenly wished he hadn't looked at all, for it was an image he was sure he would have a hard time ever forgetting and probably see in his nightmares.

He turned and looked for Starbucks. There he

was, riding in the right direction, the Krakn right behind him.

Go, Starbucks! Johnny thought, as he sped as fast as he could to reach his friend.

Johnny wove between dark, shapeless hulks in the darkness and soon they were riding side by side. Starbucks grinned in the dark.

"You got their attention all right!"

Johnny laughed. "I sure did!"

They both looked forward again and concentrated on staying on the road. Despite the danger, Johnny felt a thrill of excitement go through him. He couldn't remember ever feeling so alive before as the wind whistled past his ears. Now to let monsters meet monsters. Johnny couldn't wait to see what happened.

CHAPTER 23

Johnny and Starbucks reached the place where the wall had fallen down. Johnny peered inside. The Nork army was already there! He saw the men on their rat-beasties, dark shapes on the other side of the wall, run past the opening.

"Starbucks, look!" Johnny yelled.

Starbucks nodded grimly. "Looks like we're too late! We don't want to lead the Krakn in there, that will only make it worse!"

Johnny's mind raced. If he led the Krakn to the north gate, would he be trapping the Nork army inside, but also trapping the people of Letfreedomring? He definitely would be leading the Krakn to the people of Pelpia if he led them inside where the wall had collapsed. He decided.

"Let's still lead them to the north gate! If the Nork

army sees them coming, they may turn tail and run, and the Krakn will chase them!"

Starbucks nodded. They both rode on down the street, the Krakn right behind them. *Man, they were fast!* Johnny thought. Some of them seemed to be within arm's length, about to reach out and grab them. Johnny drove as fast as he could, his jaw tense, his eyes peeled for every roadblock ahead.

He rode on for what seemed like an eternity, but finally began to see the end of the wall ahead. As he came around to where he and Starbucks could see the front side of the north wall, Johnny saw there was still a lot of the Nork army outside the wall, waiting their turn to enter the gate.

Johnny grinned at Starbucks, who grinned back at him in the light of the yellow eye.

"Time to introduce them to each other!"

Starbucks laughed and then let out a whoop.

They rode right for the Nork army, the Krakn right behind them. There were Norkers as well as Clansmen in their skirts all mingled together. It took a moment for the Krakn to see the rat-beasties, but when they did, the immediately forgot all about Johnny and Starbucks and turned, heading right for their new prey.

Johnny and Starbucks waited until they were almost on top of the Nork army. Then they peeled off to the left. Johnny saw some of the men in the Nork army sitting on their rat-beasties turn and look at them. They saw Johnny and Starbucks and looked confused, wondering. Then they looked beyond them and saw what was coming. Their eyes went wide with surprise and mounting fear.

Johnny locked the memory of their expressions in his mind, wanting to keep it, for it was one he had a feeling he'd be cherishing for a while. Johnny and Starbucks rode far enough away to where they could stop next to a building down the street from the wall and gate and on the far side. Then they turned to watch with dark glee.

The men of Nork and their allies were caught totally by surprise as the Krakn attached. The Krakn leapt on the men and their rat-beasties, ten, twenty of them, knocking them to the ground and immediately starting to rip into them with their teeth and hold them down with their legs and arms. Quickly screams of terror and agony filled the air, and the rest of the army began to realize something terrible was happening.

Like a spreading wave, panic ensued. The Nork army turned as fast as they could and rode off back towards Nork. Some already near the gate ran inside Pelpia. It didn't' matter, for the Krakn took off after them in both directions. The Krakn leapt up to the top of the wall and bounded through the gate after them.

As Johnny watched, he thought of how unreal it all seemed, like something out of a story, not the real world. What had the world become, so full of monsters and destruction? He thought of how wild and untamed the world was, and how hard it was going to be to tame it, and yet there was something exciting, thrilling about this new world, never knowing what new monsters they had yet to face as they tried to restore Merica again. He knew they had a long, dangerous road ahead, but somehow Johnny felt as if he belonged there. This was his world now, and he wasn't afraid. He was Johnny Apocalypse, and with Misterwizard and his friends, there was nothing they couldn't fight, no battle they couldn't win.

As long as he had Deb by his side. He thought now how he wished she was by his side, watching this terrible scene unfold. She would be enjoying it just like he was, for she was just like him, full of courage and adventure. His heart suddenly gushed with love and a desire to see her again, thinking how much he loved her and was so glad she was his mate. They were made for each other.

Johnny looked over at Starbucks and saw his friend smiling too. He suspected Starbucks was lost in his own similar thoughts, maybe even thinking about Super too. They looked at each other and grinned, two adventurers in the middle of a thrilling battle.

Soon the screams of pain from both men and rat-beasties filled the air. Some of the men began firing their guns at the Krakn, and screams of pain from the Krakn, who writhed in agony and died joined the cacophony filling the night air.

The scene become something surreal, with monsters attacking monsters, and men dying and shooting weapons. Johnny and Starbucks watched, fascinated and horrified at the same time. It was terrible seeing the men and beasties die, but there was something that felt right about it as well, for it felt like justice was being served. The men had come to take what didn't belong to them, now they were getting what they deserved.

"Johnny," Starbucks said, "look at it. Who are those other people mixed in with the Norkers?"

Johnny had noticed them too. "I don't know, Starbucks. They're wearing strange clothes, like skirts or something."

"What kind of a world are we living in, now Johnny?"

Johnny grinned, realizing Starbucks was thinking a lot like he was. "A dangerous one, Starbucks, full of weird beasties and evil men. But guess what?"

"What?" Starbucks said, laughing.

"With Misterwizard's help, we're going to conquer it anyway."

"You bet we are!" Starbucks said, and they slapped hands. "I don't know about you, but I'm sure glad we left Sanctuary that day with the girls. Nothing's ever been the same."

"Me too," Johnny said, his mind going back to when they were trapped in the old, decaying place they used to live in, right there in Pelpia. It seemed like a million years ago when they lived there, and yet, he could remember it vividly. He remembered how he dreamt of leaving the dark, moldy halls and seeing what the world was like. And now that he'd been outside, he realized, just like Starbucks, that despite the ever-present danger, he was having living a life he had never even dreamt of. They may die tomorrow, Johnny thought, but at least they were alive and free today.

"Johnny, those monsters are chasing the rat-beasties and men into Pelpia!"

Starbuck's words yanked Johnny out of his reverie. "You're right. It's time we joined the fight Starbucks. Let's get inside and try to find Deb, Super and the people of Letfreedomring and give them a hand. We have to keep the Krakn busy fighting the Norkers, not our friends."

Johnny revved his engine and a second later

Starbucks did too. Then they took off together towards the open gate into Pelpia.

As Moxie watched with a dark smile, men on rattys flitted by on both sides. He passed two men on rattys standing together. The rattys' heads dipped down, eating something. As Moxie laughed, he realized it was what was left of the on the men of Letfreedomring.

Around him, rattys became distracted by the buildings and stopped to run inside some of them or sniff piles of trash that had something of interest to them. The men beat them with their clubs and pulled on the reigns, trying to get them back under control.

A ratty next to Moxie screeched, and Moxie saw it had an arrow sticking out of its neck. As Moxie watched it fell over, twitching, the man who had been riding it trapped with one leg caught underneath it. Moxie rode on, not caring if the man lived or died, enjoying himself more than he could ever remember. Everywhere around him he saw scenes of death and destruction. He saw two of his men holding one of the Letfreedomring soldiers by his arms, one on either side, dragging him out of a building. He saw another group of men lighting old pieces of cloth and throwing them inside buildings, starting them on fire and laughing.

He didn't know if he could stop the army from attacking now, they were so full of bloodlust and excitement. He would just have to wait until they had the people of Letfreedomring surrounded, and then maybe he could settle things down. Or, maybe they would all die, and that would be fine too, he thought. The evil night and the sight of all the death and destruction had turned his mind and heart cold.

He just hoped they would save the leader, what was her name, Restaria, for him. He wanted to personally take her back to the Boss as a trophy.

Suddenly he saw something up ahead. A huge pack of rattys with their riders were concentrated on a building up ahead. The building was a huge brick one with a tower at the top and what looked like some kind of metal thing in the tower. The rattys and the men of his army all crowded around the front of the building, just staring at it.

Moxie rode up. He climbed off his Harley, rolled it to where it was hidden behind a column so no one else would take it, and strode over to the large crowd of men on their rattys. Pushing his way through, he made his way to the front of the pack. And then he saw why they all stood around the building and grinned. Through the windows, he could see the men of the army of Letfreedomring peer out at them from inside. They had a big group of the Letfreedomring army trapped inside.

Moxie walked up to see Bugsy leaning on an old car, watching the mayhem ahead of him and laughing. When Moxie got close Bugsy looked at him and grinned. "Just like taking candy from a baby. Simple Simon."

Moxie grinned too. "Yeah, well maybe we better lay off. The Boss didn't say to put 'em all six feet under. He just wanted us to put the scare into 'em. Now that you got 'em surrounded, tell the guys to lay off and start looking for the dame that runs the joint."

Bugsy nodded and casually walked forward to pass on the word.

Moxie fished in his suit pocket and pulled out a silver case. Opening it, he pulled out a big, fat cigar. It was time to celebrate.

He struck a wooden match on the side of a pillar next to him and the light blazed forth, an orange glow in the darkness. He bit the end of the cigar and spit it out, put the cigar in his mouth and was about to light it, when he saw something that made him stop in mid stride.

One of his men ran up, out of breath and looking white as a ghost. He looked more scared than Moxie had ever seen anybody and he leaned on a pillar, huffing and puffing.

Mildly concerned, Moxie tried to play it cool. "What's up with you?"

Between gasps of air the man stammered out. "Monsters!"

Moxie chuckled. Monsters? This guy was nuts! But then he heard a horrid, terrifying screeching from somewhere in the darkness to the north.

"*Monsters!*" the man said, now that he had his breath. "*Monsters are attacking us! Giant spiders!*"

The man didn't wait for Moxie to reply but ran off into the darkness. Moxie heard the screeching again, and again. Suddenly his skin crawled. Something really bad was coming, something he had a feeling he didn't want to see.

He ran up to Bugsy. Bugsy and the other men had heard the screeching too, and they were all staring towards the sound, their faces drawn.

"Get ready to fight!" Moxie yelled. "Somethin's comin!"

The men didn't need him to tell them a second time. They leapt for their rattys. Those already on them turned them towards the street and started them walking. Bugsy ran back towards his and grabbed its reins, but it was scared and skittish and kept backing away from him. He disappeared into the darkness yelling obscenities as his ratty backed away and he tried to calm it down.

Moxie looked around, trying to remember where he put his Harley, but his mind was blank with terror. He ran, just to be moving, a lifeless dummy just going through the motions.

From the darkness they appeared, leaping towards him, black, four-tentacle-legged monsters with four tentacle arms, horrid shapeless mouths, a shapeless head, a hole for a nose and black beady eyes. Moxie forgot trying to be brave, for he was instantly terrified. He whimpered like a little scrabbler who had just seen a monster under his bed and tried desperately to find his Harley.

The monsters leapt over old cars and onto the sides of the buildings. They were fast and clung to the stones just like spider-beasties. Moxie forgot about the Harley, about the people of Pelpia, about everything except getting away. He ran, his mind a blank terror-filled void, away, as fast as he could.

As Moxie watched with horror, the monsters overtook his men on their rattys. The rattys went wild and took off running in all directions, the men trying to hold on. Some didn't, as they fell to the ground, the monsters were on them. They bit them with their horrible mouths and the men screamed. They ripped into the men. Blood spurted and suddenly arms and legs, and heads, came flying through the air. The men flailed on the ground in their death throes.

One of the monsters jumped on a ratty and bit its neck. It shrieked and tried to bite back, but the monster with its four arms and legs was too strong for it and the ratty couldn't get its head around to reach it. The monster ripped into the ratty and it fell. The man riding it, a Clansmen, crawled off screaming, only to be leapt upon by another monster.

What was going on? Moxie thought. Were these some kind of beasts of the people of Pelpia? If so, why didn't they bring them out earlier? No, Moxie was sure, these things weren't anyone's pets. They were attacking all on their own, a random invasion that just happened when they were fighting the Pelpians. What terrible luck!

Moxie's breathed fast, and his heart beat painfully in his chest. He no longer cared about the people of Letfreedomring, he just wanted to survive long enough to get somewhere safe. His own neck! That's all he cared about!

He ran down an empty street through the darkness, feeling the slimy tentacles of the monsters about to grab him at any second. He ran past old cars, trees and empty buildings, eyeing each dark entrance, sure one of those things was inside about to leap out at him.

He heard the screams filling the night sky, shrieks of rattys, the higher, more terrifying screams of the weird monsters, and the terrified shouts of men. Occasionally he heard gunfire. And then there would be even scarier moments of total silence, when he didn't know what was happening.

Moxie spied the rectangular opening where a door had been in the nearest building to his right. The darkness inside looked frightening, but the fear of the monsters made anything seem welcoming at the moment. He turned and ran towards it.

When he grew close, he heard voices from inside. He stopped and listened, his knees wobbly, glancing up and down the street just hoping one of the monsters didn't spy him before he could decide whether to run inside.

He realized it was the sound of women and scrabblers. It was just some of Letfreedomring's rabble, hiding out from his army. He scowled and a little of his bravado returned. He lifted his tommy gun and pointed it in front of him. He'd take some of them out, at least.

He walked inside the doorway. Even though it was dark outside, the deeper darkness inside made it hard from him to see for a moment. He waited until his eyes adjusted. Then he saw shadows, shapes in the darkness in twos and threes sitting on the floor by the walls.

People huddled together inside, holding each other. Their white eyes, wide open with fear peered at him from the blackness.

They were all hiding all right, hiding like a pack of lily-livered cowards. He grinned. He pointed his gun at them and put his finger on the trigger. He'd spray them all, just to make himself feel better.

Suddenly a blazing yellow light burst from another room. It temporarily blinded him and hurt his eyes, He shaded his eyes with his right hand and turned towards it.

"Restaria, he has a gun!"

Moxie's eyes finally adjusted and he saw to his delight that one of the women who had entered was none other than the leader dame for Letfreedomring. He had stumbled on her in the midst of all the old buildings and ruins. What luck! And even better, he had a gun trained on her. Moxie grinned. Maybe he was going to end up with Aces High after all.

CHAPTER 24

Deb ran down the dark street, feeling more and more alone. She couldn't see Deecee anywhere! She was scared, but she was determined not to lose him. She cared about him too, and the thought of him lost and hungry and all by himself spurred her to move faster. Deecee would never find her or Johnny if he kept wandering off on his own. They may never see him again.

Deb turned a corner and gasped. There stood Deecee, hunkered down and snarling, staring at two rat-beasties. On the rat-beasties two men from Nork sat, looking at Deecee. One wore a black suit and a black hat that looked like a mushroom with a bill in front. The other was really fat, and his gray suit seemed to be bursting at the seams trying to hold him in.

They laughed and pointed.

"Hey, how much ya want to bet my ratty can take it?"

"Naw, I want mine to."

"Let's let 'em both give it the business. It'll be a great show."

"All right. But if it hurts our rattys instead, we may have a long walk home."

They climbed off their rat-beasties as Deb watched in dismay. How could she save Deecee?

She looked around wildly. She had to find a way to distract them long enough for her to grab Deecee and pull him away or at least give him a chance to wander off. She decided the only thing to do was to risk herself.

She walked forward until the two men saw her. Instantly they forgot about Deecee, their mouths open with surprise and interest.

"Hey, look, a dame!"

"And what a dame! Hey Toots, come over here!"

Deb smiled darkly and slowly backed away.

The men took off running after her! That wasn't what she'd hoped for! Now Deecee was alone with those rat-beasties, and the men were right behind her!

She ran fast, her long blond hair flowing in the night air. She was young and fast, and she darted down the dark, litter filled street. The men were fast too though, and they were bigger and stronger. They came after her, two hulking dark fearsome shapes gliding after her.

Deb wondered about Deecee as she ran as fast as she could, looking around for a place to hide. Fear filled her mind but she tried to fight it and concentrate on getting away.

She spotted an open doorway and darted inside. The interior was pitch black, and she wondered if she'd just done something really dumb, for she had to stop, afraid of running into something. She heard the men talking to each other outside and ran to the right, her hands out in front of her to feel anything she might bump into.

The men were right outside.

"You see where she went?"

"Naw. Look, we better get back and see what's happenin' with our rattys. That doggie might be killing 'em right now."

"But did you see that dame? I'll take her over my ratty, even if I have to walk home."

"Find her on your own, then," the other one said. "I'm missing a good fight."

"Yeah, I bet you're right. Too bad though. She was definitely a hot tomato."

With relief, Deb heard their voices fade as the men walked back to their rattys. She was worried about Deecee though; did she even help him, or did those horrid rat-beasties kill him? She hated to go back and risk being captured again, but she didn't see much choice if she wanted to save Deecee.

Slowly she peeked out the doorway. She didn't see the men anywhere, but she could hear their voices, now seeming far away. She slowly followed them, wondering what had happened to Deecee.

Johnny and Starbucks sped down the street past the dark buildings on either side, green with vegetation, looking sinister and bizarre in the night. They passed a side street where they saw two Krakn busy eating something, but they didn't stop to see what. They passed a group of three of the strange soldiers with the skirts standing over the dead body of a Krakn. Lying next to it lay a dead rat-beastie.

Johnny scowled and stopped his Harley. Starbucks saw and did too. Johnny hopped off and took his sword out. Starbucks looked at Johnny's face and saw the fury on it.

Johnny whispered to him, "Let's find out who

these guys are, and why they're helping the Norkers."

Starbucks nodded and took his sword out of his belt too, feeling just as cold and deadly. It was time to pay the invaders back for bringing death and destruction on the innocent people of Letfreedromring. They advanced on the Nork men, crouched, their swords in front of them.

The strange men wore the skirts and had on heavy boots. They too had white shirts and sashes over their shoulders. One had a cigar in their mouth like the type Misterwizard smoked. One had a tommy gun, another held a heavy stone hatchet, and the third held a wooden club.

Johnny and Starbucks walked as silently as they could, trying to get as close as possible before they were spotted. They reached within three feet before the man smoking the cigar with the hatchet saw them. His mouth opened and the cigar fell out of his mouth. He saw Johnny and Starbucks' swords in their hands. He was just about to yell when Johnny's sword stabbed him in the chest. He grabbed the wound, dropped his hatchet and fell to the ground, blood pouring from the cut.

The man with the tommy gun turned and fired. Johnny and Starbucks dove in opposite directions, and bullets sprayed the street. The end of the tommy gun flashed yellow in the darkness as the man turned it in all directions, trying to hit them.

Johnny dove to the ground and rolled as a spray of bullets erupted right where he'd been. The man with a club took off after Starbucks, but being black and in his dark pants, it was hard to see Starbucks in the dark. The man crept along, trying to see him, swinging his club in an arc, as if Starbucks was going to rush him at any moment.

Starbucks leapt out of the darkness and swung his sword in a deadly arc. The Clansman with the club yelled and raised his club at the last moment. The sword hit it with a dull thud and embedded itself in the wood. Starbucks tried to pull it back, but it was stuck. The man grimaced a smile and did a sweep kick at Starbuck's legs.

Starbucks went down and the man was on him. The man was bigger than Starbucks who was still only seventeen seasons old. The weight of the man pinned him down as the man rained blows on Starbucks' body.

But what he lacked in size Starbucks made up for in determination and courage. Soon Starbucks was kicking and punching the man back, and they rolled around on the ground. The sword and club, stuck together were dropped and they both used their fist to fight the other.

Meanwhile, the man with the tommy gun chased Johnny, enjoying himself. He passed by dark buildings, straining his eyes to try and see which one Johnny might have ran into.

"Come on out, ya little Mousie. Let Harry give you a little bit a cheese, right from this here tommy gun. I ken ya for missing with the Clan."

Johnny tried to keep something between him and the man with the tommy gun, his sword ready for a chance to get close enough to strike. The man seemed confident, almost relaxed, knowing he had the advantage with his gun against Johnny's sword.

From the shadows, Johnny's voice floated in the air. "Who are you people, and why are you helping the Norkers?"

The man smiled, knowing he was close to his prey. "We be the Clan, young laddie, and we only help ourselves. Now you surrender yourself and do yourself a wee favor. I promise to treat ya fairly, and that's my solemn oath."

Johnny didn't answer, and the man tried to gauge where Johnny's voice had come from. He walked that direction.

"You got a wee more guts than most of these pipsqueaks here, I'll give ya that," the man said, as he peered into the darkness and searched around.

He passed an old street lamp, the glass bulb long since gone, and an old metal box with a round top that had once been a mailbox. He stopped after he walked around each object, leery of Johnny and his sword, knowing that even with his gun, if this strange boy in leather pants and vest with his short yellow hair could still kill him if he wasn't careful.

The man began to grow impatient at not finding Johnny, and even a little bit worried that Johnny was going to get the drop on him. He clenched his jaw and stopped moving. He peered around in the dark, looking for the slightest change in the darkness around him.

Then he saw it, a dark shape in the distance. He grinned. He'd found his quarry. He moved slowly forward. Yes, there was the boy, waiting for him at the end of the street, his sword in his hand.

The man cautiously moved towards the boy, leery of a trap. The boy just stood there, not moving. Was he giving up? Did he think the man would capture him as a prisoner? If that was the case, the man thought with dark pleasure the kid was in for a big surprise. Oath or no oath, the lad had just stabbed the man's partner. There was no way this wee one was gonna go anywhere except full of holes.

The boy was inside an old one-story building whose roof was gone and the sides were mostly caved in. The boy stood at the back of the building on a pile of old rubble. The man stopped just outside the door. He waited, but he didn't see anything suspicious. The boy just stood there, sword pointed at the ground, staring daggers at him.

The man smiled. "You be a smart lad. Surrender, and we'll make it easy on ya. You're not a bad fighter. Maybe you can join the Clan. You can have a kilt and a sash of your own. Would ya like that, now?"

The boy just smiled grimly and stared at him. It made the man's skin crawl. What was he up to?

The kid was crazy, that was it, the man realized. He had been out here on his own all his life, and was just a wild kid without any understanding of living among civilized people. It made the man warm inside. It was gonna be fun killing this kid, and really, he was doing everybody a favor.

He stepped inside one foot. Nothing happened. The boy didn't move. He looked around. There was nothing there. He pulled back the bolt on his tommy gun, making a loud cracking sound. He aimed.

Then he saw the boy grin even wider. The boy looked up above him, behind him to the man's left. The man turned and looked up.

There on the wall clung one of the Krakn. As the man screamed and turned his gun towards it, the Krakn leapt on him. As it bit the man, he shot his tommy gun, the bullets hitting the far wall and spraying rock and debris.

Johnny smiled and leapt over the broken wall as the Krakn finished its gruesome meal.

Starbucks and the man he fought rolled over and over, kicking and hitting. Finally, the man began to see that Starbucks, though younger, was a better fighter and had a lot more speed and toughness than he did. As Starbucks continued to punch and kick him the man crawled away and tried to get to his feet. Starbucks stopped long enough to get up, but that was enough for the man to crawl five feet away. As Starbucks ran after him, the man leapt up and ran off into the darkness, his face bloody and beaten.

Starbucks stopped, his own face covered with blood and bruises. He leaned over, tired and sore, and put his hands on his knees.

When he caught his breath, he stood up with a grin. "That'll teach ya a lesson, creep. Nobody messes with Starbucks!"

Starbucks laughed and whooped in victory. Then he staggered over to pull his sword from the man's club.

Johnny walked up, looking cocky and cheerful, and Starbuck knew he must have beaten his man too.

"They called themselves, 'the Clan,'" Johnny said.

Starbucks just grinned. They walked up to each other and smiled in victory. Then just for old time's sake,

Johnny slugged Starbucks on the shoulder. Starbucks winced, remembering their old game. He slugged Johnny back in the chest. They both laughed, put their arms over each other's shoulders, and walked back to their Harleys.

CHAPTER 25

Super ran off into the darkness. Somehow, she'd become saddled with a whole group of scrabblers, ten of them, with no parents. They were all scared and gazed around at the darkness. The oldest couldn't be more than ten seasons, and the youngest looked like she was only four.

Super didn't like being in charge of the little children, it made her feel anxious, desperate to make sure she didn't let anything happen to them. She put her hands on the shoulders of the two nearest to her and tried to keep them moving.

"Keep quiet, and just move nice and steady towards that big building over there," Super said, looking at it so they'd know which one she was talking about. "Once we're all inside and hidden, I'll go find your parents."

Super led the group along the sidewalk next to the street. Dark shapes loomed everywhere, and the mold and grass covering the ground and the buildings gave everything a creepy look.

Everything they passed seemed to scare the children. One of the young boys started crying, and it caught on quickly. It wasn't long before another, then another joined in.

"Where's my mommy?" A little girl asked between sobs.

"I'm scared," a little black girl said as she gazed around. She reminded Super of Sephie and her heart went out to her. "Are we going to be captured?"

"We're all a little scared," Super said. "But don't worry. The men of the army are going to protect us. We just have to be smart and hide so that they don't have to worry about us."

A ten-season-old boy glared at Super. "You don't even know where you're taking us."

Super glared back in the darkness. "Just do what I say, please. We don't have time for arguing."

The boy puffed himself up. "I can take care of these scrabblers. They're my people, not yours."

Super felt insulted and grew irritated. The last thing she needed was an insurrection. "I'm here to help. And I'm older than you, so..."

"We should be taking them to the big building with the lion-beasties out front. It's got lots of rooms, and the stairs go down to great places to hide."

"Really?" Super said. "That's nice, but we don't have time to take a long walk. We have to hide now, and these scrabblers can't make it very far."

The boy pointed. "It's just one street over. You can see the top of it from here."

Super looked where he was pointing. In the dark between the buildings, she could see a black shape that seemed to tower up and fill the sky.

Super shrugged. She turned to the other children. "Scrabblers, do you think you could make it to that building okay?"

The children, seeing that there was some sort of plan, seemed to cheer up a little. Small heads nodded and Super even saw a smile or two looking at her from the darkness.

Super turned to the boy. "Okay, lead the way."

The boy smiled, feeling important and like he'd won. He reminded Super of Johnny a little, and she thought that he looked like he'd be a courageous fighter for his people someday, maybe.

The boy took off at a fast pace.

"Hey! Wait for us!"

They all shuffled across the street then down the

alley between two buildings. Here there was lots of trash and metal boxes on wheels. Super and the scrabblers hurried to keep up with the boy, but the children all seemed terrified and it was all Super could do to keep them going. They heard the squeak of rat-beasties, ordinary sized ones, and somewhere an old wildie sat in the dark singing to himself. Even Super felt icky as they crept along the slimy, moss-covered street. The buildings seemed to crowd in on either side, with ledges that led to large doors.

Super kept moving the scrabblers along, her heart beating hard, wondering if going down the narrow passageway after the boy was the best idea after all. Finally, after what seemed like an eternity, they reached the other side. The boy was going to run out right away, but Super whispered loudly "Wait!"

The boy stopped and looked at her impatiently. She ignored him and instead peered up the street in both directions, making sure the coast was clear.

Suddenly from the left came a huge group of soldiers. They were just dark figures in a large bunch running swiftly. Super grabbed the boy and pulled him back into the darkness. Then they all watched the soldiers' approach.

As they grew close, Super could tell they were men of Letfreedomring. They looked haggard and dirty, and many had blood on their faces and clothing. They carried clubs and swords. Some were wounded, being carried along by others.

As they began to pass, Super could tell they'd been in some kind of battle. They ran as fast as they could, which worried Super, for it made her think something was chasing them, and she was sure she knew what it was.

Thirty or forty men ran by. They didn't appear to be trying to fight anything, just hurry and get away as fast as they could.

The last one passed by on the left, disappearing into the darkness. Super knew this was their only chance. She turned to the boy.

Super turned to the boy leader. "Something's chasing them! We need to get the scrabblers over there now!"

The boy nodded bravely. Super realized she was beginning to like this kid, he had guts. The boy ran out into the street, motioning with his hand. Super pushed the children along, and as fast as they could they hurried across the street.

Just as the boy said, two huge shapes sitting on stone blocks stood on either side of the stairs leading towards the entrance. In the dark it was hard to see what they were, but Super was sure they were the lion-beasties the boy had talked about.

Quickly they all ran up the stone steps. The steps were wide so they had to run and jump, run and jump. Super glanced around, and wasn't happy at how exposed they were. As she ran, she peered off to their right, straining her ears and looking as sharply as she could, hoping they had enough time to get inside before whatever was coming arrived. She had been at the wall with Restaria and Deb, but she'd stayed down below and never really gotten a look at what the Nork army looked like. She had a feeling she wasn't going to like it when she did see.

One of the little girls was of Asian descent, just like Lightpole, and plump. She was dressed in handmade pants and a shirt made out of pieces of different colored cloth and cloth shoes. She didn't seem scared at all, and was skipping from one stair to the next, then stopping and looking at the stairs for a moment then jumping again. Just what Super didn't need. Super hurried over to get her moving faster. Then she saw two of the boys were chasing each other in circles, laughing and yelling. Super groaned inwardly and remembered why she hated it when she was chosen to watch the scrabblers back at Sanctuary.

"Hey!" she whispered loudly. "Get inside now, before I paddle all your behinds!"

They all looked at her and laughed, ignoring her. The boy leader grinned at her and turned to the scrabblers. "Everybody inside, now!"

They all immediately stopped what they were doing and obeyed. Super grinned. This kid was a lot like Johnny, for the others already listened to him.

Suddenly they heard a horrible squeaking sound from the darkness to their right. It was a creepy, inhuman sound that made Super's blood run cold.

She turned to the scrabblers. "Hurry!"

They all listened this time and ran faster towards the huge doors into the building.

Super turned and looked again, and this time she saw something that made her even more upset than the sound.

A man hobbled along, leaning on a pole. His leg was bleeding and his clothes were covered with sweat and blood. With shock Super realized it was Lightpole! He was the last to leave the battle, but he was wounded.

"Daddy!" The little Asian girl pointed at Lightpole with a look of concern.

Super turned to the ten-year-old boy leader. "What's your name?"

He stood up straight and with arrogance. "My name is Redeye."

"Great," Super said, rolling her eyes. "Listen

Redeye, you seem to be a brave and smart kid, I mean boy. Can you take charge of the scrabblers and keep them safe?"

"Sure, I can!" Redeye said, puffing out his chest.

"Good! Then take them inside, and help them hide until somebody comes to get you!"

Redeye nodded and right away began leading the children towards the entrance. Super breathed deeply, not really wanting to do what she was about to do, but knowing she didn't have a choice. Then she ran back down the steps to help Lightpole.

And she was just in time, for from the darkness, the first men on their rat-beasties appeared. They stepped along clumsily, as if having trouble keeping the rat-beasties from going off in different directions. Every few seconds a rat-beastie would stop and look around, and the man sitting on it would club it on the side until it would start to run again. But they were still coming.

Super ran down and put her head under Lightpole's arm. He saw her and grinned, but then he grimaced in pain. Super put her arm around him and lifted up his weight. Together they moved faster.

Lightpole wheezed and said in a raspy voice, "You should not be here! You are endangering yourself!"

"Hush!" Super said. "Save your strength for walking, unless you want to be rat-beastie food."

Lightpole grinned, despite his pain. "No, that I do not."

Suddenly they heard the bell of Bell House ringing.

"Restaria is gathering the people. We must hurry! Together they moved as fast as they could down the street, the Nork army not far behind them.

Deb stared out at the dark, empty city, just row after row of empty shells with deserted streets. She couldn't remember ever feeling so alone and defeated before. Everyone she knew was off somewhere in the distance, separated, fighting battles, and she was all by herself. Somewhere in the dark, monsters were on every side. Two evil men still searched for her. And now she'd lost Deecee. She suddenly felt bone-tired, and leaned on the brick wall of a one-story building. It had once had a huge glass window, but it was long since shattered. Pieces of the window lay inside next to old shelves and piles of junk, all buried under a hundred-year-old pile of dust and vegetation.

Looking into the building made her feel even more alone, as if trapped in a bizarre wonderland where nothing was real anymore. Everywhere she looked, the yellow eye illuminated the vegetation clinging to the buildings like an evil growth. The cars in the streets were like dark, hulking shadows buried under a century of dirt and mold.

She shook her head to clear it, for she began to think if she kept on like she was, she was going to become a wildie too. She could understand how being all alone in this stark, barren city could drive someone crazy.

The cold night wind whipped her long blond hair up in the back as if she was sailing on a cloud. She shivered, for her jeans, cotton shirt and leather jacket didn't do much to keep out the cold.

She took one more look down the street, and realized that she had to give up looking for Deecee. He could be anywhere, and she needed to get back to someone she knew, for hunger and exhaustion would soon set in and she didn't need to get too weak to defend herself.

"Deecee, please come back," she said softly, without hope. There was no answer except the howling of the wind. No bark, no sound of people talking, no sound at all.

She looked around and tried to orient herself. Suddenly she realized she didn't really know which way was back to Restaria and Super. The thought alarmed her and her heart beat wildly as panic started to take hold. She scowled and fought it down. The last thing she needed was to wander off without thinking, scaring herself more and more as she tried to find some kind of landmark.

She took a deep breath and started walking, studying the buildings. She tried to retrace her steps, but at the last when she was running from the men, she really didn't have time to look where she was going.

Suddenly she heard a sound that filled her with relief. It was the bell in Bell House ringing, the sound drifting on the night air like an invisible living thing. It seemed miles away, but she was sure she could tell that the sound came from somewhere to her left. She smiled and walked quickly towards it. Suddenly she felt like weeping, and crossly berated herself for being such a scaredy-cat.

Her heart still beat wildly though, and inside fear kept trying to keep hold as her mind told her she was never going to find the bell, not before she grew too tired or weak.

"Stop it!" she whispered to herself. "Are you Deb, Johnny's girl or not? Stop being such a little scrabbler." Her words were meant to encourage herself, but somehow hearing her voice in the dark just made her feel more afraid. She decided to keep quiet until she could show herself a landmark. That would stop the fear right in its tracks. She hurried along, walking down the moss-covered street, keeping a wary eye on every building, mad at Deecee for getting her into this mess in the first place.

CHAPTER 26

oxie grinned with pleasure at the men and women cowering in front of him. Restaria stared at him sullenly, but with fear, knowing that her and her people were trapped by the leader of the Norkers. It made Moxie feel wonderful, excited, in power. It was the feeling he craved most, the feeling of having everyone look at him with fear, like he was somebody to be reckoned with. He stood there, wanting to prolong the moment as long as he could, for he wasn't sure right then if he and his army were going to win or lose. All he knew was, at least he could get some really good revenge.

"Please listen to me," Restaria said. "We were perfectly willing to give you tribute, but you didn't give us a chance. Whatever we have you can take. How can your king continue to get tribute from us if you kill us?

Her words sent Moxie into a rage, as if he could

lecture her on policy. His lip curled and he pointed his tommy gun at her, which made the people of Pelpia gasp.

"Shut yer trap or I'll shut it for ya. You think you was smart, sendin' those freaky monsters to put the kibosh on us. But we ain't that easy to kill, sister. Now it's you people's turn for some dyin' and some screamin'!"

The people of Pelpia yelled and huddled together at his words, staring up at him with fright.

Restaria stepped closer to Moxie, not showing fear, though there was sorrow in her eyes at what he might do. "We didn't send those monsters after you. They came from the city to the south called Balmor. They killed our people too. Please, give us a chance to show you we can cooperate."

"Show you we can cooperate," Moxie mocked. "I'll show you how I can cooperate."

Moxie pointed his gun at a woman lying on the floor, her arms around her little frightened girl. The people of Pelpia screamed in terror and tried to crawl further away. The woman and little girl sat still, staring with terror at him and his tommy gun.

"No!" Restaria yelled, putting her hand up. Moxie turned the gun on her.

"Another move, lady, and they all get it. I got to show you we mean business."

"Then kill me instead! I'm the leader. It was my fault!"

Moxie scowled with distaste. "I hate goody-two-shoe types like you. Always actin' like you're so noble, sacrificin' yerselves. And everybody's supposed to think you're so wonderful, and makin' me look like a lousey. All right. You want to die instead?"

Moxie pulled back the bolt of his tommy gun and aimed it at Restaria. The people all yelled and wept, knowing she was about to die.

Suddenly the door burst open. Everyone turned to see who it was.

It was Bugsy, Moxie's second in command.

"Hey Moxie! I heard you in here!"

Moxie forgot about Restaria for the moment and turned to look at Bugsy. "So, what's the score? Are we all dead?"

Bugsy looked tired and dirty, his face shining with sweat. He held his gun towards the floor, as if it was too heavy to lift.

"Not all of us. A lot a guys high-tailed it away with those things chasin' 'em. We managed to kill a few. But there ain't none of 'em around right now. We got to cheese it, before they come back!"

Moxie grinned, the wheels in his head turning. "Okay. Okay. We gonna cheese it all right. But we're taking these people with us."

Bugsy looked at the people and Restaria, then back to Moxie. "Takin' 'em with us?"

"Yeah. They gonna be our insurance that those things don't attack again. And if they do, we'll feed 'em them so we can escape."

Bugsy grinned. The people of Letfreedomring murmured with fear.

"But if you take us with you, how can we pay you tribute?"

"You let me worry about that, sweetheart. I think the Boss will be just as happy with some slaves."

Bugsy chuckled, and Moxie joined him.

"Everybody outside, now!" Moxie motioned with his gun. The people of Letfreedomring slowly rose up, talking to each other in frightened tones. Moxie turned his gun back on Restaria.

"Ain't gonna be any trouble is there, queenie?"

Restaria stared daggers at him, but she knew there was nothing she could do, at the moment. She smiled primly and began to help the people get up and walk outside.

Outside, they found thirty or forty men of the Nork army standing around next to their rat-beasties. Most had guns but a few had swords or clubs, dark with blood from the recent battle. They looked tired and haggard. Some were covered with blood and dirt and few had bandaged arms or heads. They all glanced around nervously, searching for more monsters. When they saw Moxie, they all started talking at once.

"Moxie! We gotta get out of here!"

"Moxie, them things is comin' back!"

"Moxie, hey Moxie!"

Moxie put up a hand. "Simmer down! Quiet down!"

His men all stopped talking and stared at him, but they continued to be on edge.

Moxie looked at the small group of Letfreedomring people huddled together for protection, with Restaria at the front.

"Not very much of a prize," Bugsy said, "'specially after losin' so many of our guys."

"Yeah," Moxie said. He thought for a moment, then he smiled. He looked in the direction of Bell House

"So, let's get a bigger one. It's time for a town meeting. Bugsy, remember that building we passed where we had the men trapped?"

Bugsy looked at it and back at Moxie with a smile of interest. "Yeah."

"What happened to the men you had inside?"

Bugsy grinned with evil. "We shot 'em all, Moxie."

The people all wailed in grief, and Moxie smiled

with evil joy.

"That's just great, Bugsie." Moxie pointed. "Now listen. Inside is some kinda thing they make noise with. They pull on a rope and it makes a lotta racket. I heard 'em use it earlier. I think it's how they gather everybody together."

Bugsy grinned with dark glee. "Then let's gather 'em together, ay Moxie?" He ran over to some men and lead them towards the building.

Restaria frowned. "If you ring our bell, it may attract more of those monsters!"

"You better hope it don't, sister," Moxie replied. "'Cause you guys are who they's gonna feed on if it does."

"Our army will never let you take us away," Restaria said coldly.

Moxie scowled at her. "There ain't much of yer army left, sister. And whatever is, better not cause trouble if they don't wanna see a lot of dead citizens. I wouldn't worry about your 'army' anymore. I don't think there's enough left to lead a funeral procession."

Restaria glared at Moxie. He grinned back, enjoying her reaction.

After a few minutes, they all heard the bell of Bell House ring, filling the night air with its melodious sound.

Moxie and his men led Restaria and their

prisoners back towards Bell House, pointing their guns at the darkness, waiting for the people of Letfreedomring to show up.

Johnny and Starbucks rode slowly, looking all around for signs of battle going on so they could help the men of Letfreedomring.

In the darkness next to a tall, gray building to his right, Johnny saw a Krakn run by. Its black shape seemed huge in the darkness, and its four horrible legs moved swiftly as it ran. Johnny felt a chill run up and down his spine, and in his mind the thought popped up, *Be glad it didn't see you.* The desire to run and hide came over him, and like he always did, he had to force it down and take control of his nerves. It was a constant battle to stay courageous in the face of danger, and sometimes he wasn't sure he was going to win the fight. He wondered if anyone knew how scared he was sometimes and if it showed.

He looked over at Starbucks and was cheered to see fear on his face too as he looked at where the Krakn was. It made Johnny feel closer to his friend, that they were facing the danger together.

"We should follow that Krakn and make sure it

doesn't attack anyone from Letfreedomring."

"Yeah," Starbucks said wryly. "Let's follow that monster and see if we can get its attention."

Suddenly they heard yelling and the sound of fighting. Without a word they both turned their Harleys towards the sounds and sped up.

The sound came from a side street up ahead. Johnny and Starbucks sped up until they could see down the street. There they saw five Nork army men standing next to three rat-beasties. They stood next to a one-story brick building and peered inside. They grinned, and it looked like they had someone trapped inside.

Knowing it had to be someone from Letfreedomring, Johnny yelled, "Let's go help them!" They both turned down the street and sped toward the fight.

As they grew close, they stopped their Harleys and climbed off. Both Johnny and Starbucks took out their swords and ran towards the Nork soldiers, who hadn't spotted them yet.

As they drew close, they heard the Nork soldiers talking.

"Come on out, or we're sending out rattys in to get you!"

From inside came a gruff reply. "Come in and fight us like men, you cowardies!"

Johnny recognized the voice. It was Jewelrydept!

"You have the guts to do your own fighting?"

It was Bargainbin too.

"We'd rather see our rattys have some fun," one of the men said, as the rest chuckled. "How fast can you run, bud?"

Johnny and Starbucks reached the men, and they turned just in time to see Johnny, sword raised, swing it down in a deadly arc. The man he was aiming at was hit on the shoulder, and he fell backwards on the ground with a gash oozing blood. The rest of the men raised their clubs and swords. The fight was on.

As the remaining Norkers ran to fight Johnny and Starbucks, Jewelrydept and Bargainbin saw what was happening from inside. They ran out to help. Jewelrydept had a sharpened stick in his hand but all Bargainbin had was a large chuck of rock.

The Nork soldiers ran at Johnny and Starbucks and the boys had to back up, being outnumbered two to one. But it wasn't long before the odds were even, for two of the Nork soldiers had to turn and face Jewelrydept and Bargainbin as they came at them from behind.

The rat-beasties looked alarmed and backed away. One turned and began to waddle off. Johnny and Starbucks fought the men attacking them, warding off their blows and trying to land ones of their own.

Jewelrydept had to be careful, for the man he fought had a club and he swung it over and over, trying to knock the stick Jewelrydept held out of his hand. Jewelrydept kept moving out of the way, then thrusting the stick in, trying to stab the man in the arm to make him drop his weapon.

Bargainbin would have been doing worse, if it wasn't for the fact that he managed to hit his adversary on the head with the rock before the man could even turn towards him. A trickle of blood ran down the back of the man's head, and as he tried to focus on Bargainbin, he staggered, woozy, his eyes having a hard time focusing.

"Not so tough now, are ya guys?" Bargainbin taunted, circling his opponent and trying to find a place where he could land another blow.

Suddenly Jewelrydept's opponent hit him on the wrist. Jewelrydept yelled and he dropped his stick. The man laughed and advanced on him, but Jewelrydept rushed him. Hitting him in the midsection, both men went down onto the hard pavement where they punched and kicked at each other, rolling around.

Johnny was a better fighter than his enemy, and he found a way in and slashed the man on the cheek, leaving a dark red gash that began to bleed immediately.

The man's eyes opened wide in fear and he turned and ran off into the night, believing discretion the better part of valor.

Johnny grinned and turned to help Starbucks, but he really didn't need it. His opponent circled him, sweat pouring from his forehead despite the cool of the night, his face showing fear and his club held before him. Starbucks was having fun with the man, circling and jabbing, not really trying to stab him, just trying to play on the man's fears.

The man looked and saw Johnny's opponent run off. It seemed their courage only lasted as long as they had their enemy outnumbered, for now he too took off running.

Johnny and Starbucks, winded, took a moment to catch their breath. Then they ran over to help the other two men with their fight.

They found Bargainbin standing over the inert body of his opponent, who lay on the concrete unconscious. He had an even bigger cut on his chin where Bargainbin had hit him good.

They all turned to see Jewelrydept still on the ground fighting his opponent. Johnny began to move towards the fight, but Bargainbin grabbed his arm.

"Let them fight, Johnny," Bargainbin said smiling. "Don't worry, Jewelrydept is strong and tough. It won't be long."

Sure enough, as they watched Jewelrydept began to get the advantage, raining blow after blow on his opponent until the man stopped struggling and just put his hands up to his face to protect it.

Jewelrydept kept hitting him, blow after blow, until the man stopped moving altogether, whether out of fear or because he was no longer conscious. When he realized his opponent was no longer fighting back, Jewelrydept finally let him go. The man slumped onto the ground, his mouth open and bruises already forming all over his face.

Jewelrydept got up, and Bargainbin ran to him. They hugged and then turned to face Johnny and Starbucks.

"You guys can handle yourselves pretty good!" Starbucks laughed.

"We could have taken two of them, but not the whole group," Jewelrydept said. "Thank you for helping us."

"Now we truly know you two are not like Leader Nordstrom," Bargainbin said. "We're your friends forever."

"And we're yours," Johnny said. "But I don't think we have time to talk about it right now."

"Yes!" Jewelrydept said. "Let's go find some

more of our people who need help!"

As if in response, the quiet night air was split by a distant ringing. All four men turned towards the sound.

"It's Bell House," Jewelrydept said. "Restaria is gathering the people."

"The battle must be happening there!" Bargainbin said.

Johnny and Starbucks hurried towards their Harleys.

"You guys need a ride?" Johnny said.

Jewelrydept and Bargainbin looked at each other and smiled.

"No thank you," Bargainbin said. "We've always wanted to try and ride one of these rat-beasties. Now's our chance."

Johnny and Starbucks laughed. "Good luck!" Starbucks said. They jumped on their Harleys, flipped the kickstands and took off.

"Once more…" Johnny started.

"Into the breech!" Starbucks finished. "One day you're going to have to tell me what that even means."

"Like I know," Johnny yelled back.

They took off as Jewelrydept and Bargainbin walked towards two of the rat-beasties gingerly, scared but excited to try and ride the strange creatures.

CHAPTER 27

eb ran swiftly down the dark, dirty street, feeling totally alone. No matter how brave she tried to be, she felt as if she was somehow floating in a dark world where a monster could jump out of one of the moss-covered buildings or from inside one of the moldy hulks of steel in the street. The night was cold, and she felt the chill down to her bones. She couldn't help feeling the loss of Deecee, and still hoped that at any moment he would come loping towards her from the shadows. What a warm and friendly sight that would be!

She didn't know what she was running to either. Had the Letfreedomring won the battle, and they were gathering together in victory, or was Restaria trying to gather the people together to flee?

Deb stopped running, out of breath. The yellow eye shone down on the crumbling buildings around her, covered with hanging moss. The streets were covered with grass and moss, and it looked like the vegetation was slowly engulfing the whole world. The buildings didn't seem to have any difference now, just some a little taller than others but all covered with coats of green.

As she walked, she was careful, for some of the moss underneath her feet was slippery. She could still hear the bell from Bell House, its bong, bong sound somehow scary in the darkness. Each peel made her heart jump, as if she was afraid something bad was going to hear it, and she wanted more than anything to run away from it, but here she was, walking into who knew what danger.

She reached an intersection of two streets, and as she walked around the corner of the buildings, the bell sounded louder. She could tell which direction it was coming from now, to her left. She turned and started up the street.

Suddenly she felt calmer for some reason. She was moving towards other people at least, and she wouldn't be so alone. She sighed and tried to cheer herself up. Somewhere out there was Johnny, fighting the bad men, and soon he and Deb would be reunited. The thought of running into Johnny's arms, throwing her arms around his neck and planting kiss after kiss on him filled her with a quiet joy. He was her mate. How lucky she was! No matter what happened, they would always love each other, and she would always have him to share adventures with. How she wished she was in his arms right then!

Suddenly a huge, dark figure ran out from the doorway of a windowless building to her right. The building had a sign that said, "Drugstore," but the sign was tilted and covered with green dirt.

Deb screamed but before she could even react, the figure came at her and grabbed her wrist. Terror filled her as she struggled wildly to get free. She could tell now that the figure was a man, but he was dressed funny in a green and black checkered skirt and a dirty white shirt that was untucked in the front. He wore a red and green checkered sash across his chest and wore big, heavy boots.

His was a big man, with a large square face, black hair and a black beard. He wore an evil grin, and he was taller than her. His hand was big and strong, and his grip hurt her arm.

She twisted her arm, but his grip was like an iron vise. She kicked him wildly, connecting with his shin. He yelled something and moved his leg back as she tried to kick it again. She slugged at him with her free hand. Then he laughed.

"Got a little tiger here, do I?" the man said. His

voice had a strange accent that she didn't recognize. Then he just stood there as she kicked and slugged at him, not even being fazed by it, and Deb felt humiliated as she ran out of energy and he grinned at her, his yellow teeth gleaming in the light of the yellow eye.

"My, but you're quite a dish, ain't ya lassie?' His accent had a lilt to it, like he came from some foreign land. "Let's have a wee bit of fun, you and Clancy, how you feel about that?"

Deb, her face flushed, spit in his face.

The bell rung again, seeming close now. They both looked towards the sound.

"I kairn that something be happening, lassie. Lucky for you my time is fleeting, or I'd show you how good it is to be with a man from the Clan. Let's go have a gander and see what old Moxie is up to, shall we?"

He strode along, dragging Deb with him, his iron grip hurting her and making her feel woozy. They walked around a building to see a rat-beastie standing there, its reigns tied to an old lamppost. Its saddle was different, with a green and red blanket under it in a checkered pattern.

"This here be Annabelle. She's a sweetheart, if you like dirty, stinky rattys. Normally us Clansmen like good old fashioned horsies. But this is what these filthy Norkers ride, so we have to play along. Don't you worry though, she'll get us where we're going in a jiffy."

The man led her up to the rat-beastie, grabbed her waist and threw her on. She yelped and wrinkled her nose, but at least he let go of her wrist which ached.

Before she had a chance to hop off again, the man jumped on behind and wrapped his arms around her waist, securing her tight.

"Are you part of the Nork army?" Deb asked, for he didn't talk the way the Norkers did.

"I be Clancy McTavvin. We be the Clan. We live to the north of Nork, but we align ourselves with the Norkers from time to time, when it suits us."

Deb shook her head. There were so many different peoples up north here, she was tired of trying to keep track of them, let alone try to understand all the weird ways they all talked. It seemed the King of Nork had lots of allies, which was very bad. It meant he would be harder to defeat.

"Get along Annabelle," Clancy said He kicked Annabelle in the side and she began to trot along towards the sound of the bell.

"We may be heading for a bit of a skirmish, lassie. But don't you worry your pretty little head about it. If we find a storm up ahead, I'll just point ole Annabelle to home and take you for myself."

Deb scowled and tried to pry his fingers loose

with hers, but his grip was like steel. She could no more move them than a block of concrete. What had she gotten herself into? Where was Johnny?

To Moxie's delight, not only the people of Letfreedomring began to assemble, but riding out of the darkness were men from his army on their rat-beasties and a few of the Clansmen as well. As soon as the people of Letfreedomring saw Moxie and his soldiers holding Restaria captive, they tried to turn and run, but quickly Nork soldiers grabbed them and led them into the square in front of Bell House. Soon there was more than a hundred frightened townspeople standing in a circle, women, men and scrabblers all staring around with fright. Some of the Letfreedomring soldiers were there too, wounded or just plain looking defeated.

Moxie walked up to one of his soldiers who climbed off his rat-beastie to report.

"Where are them monsters?" Moxie asked him.

The man pointed out into the darkness. "We killed some. Others are chasing our guys all over the place." The man's eyes opened wide with worry. "But they'll hear the sound, Moxie. We got to cheese it fast, before they find us."

Moxie nodded and turned to Restaria.

"What are you going to do with us?" Restaria asked, looking at Moxie with a dark, steady gaze. "You surely don't expect us all, women and scrabblers, to walk to Nork."

Moxie grinned. "Well sister, that's exactly what I expect. Don't worry, once we leave this city, we'll take a break or two. We don't want our tribute dyin' before the Boss sees it."

"You can't do this!" Restaria said, moving forward slightly and spreading her hands open in supplication. "Please, we have tribute to give you. You never gave us a chance!"

"We ain't got no more time to wait. Now," he said, pointing his tommy gun at her. "You gonna give 'em the order, or am I gonna do it? If I do it, I promise ya it won't be so gentle-like."

Restaria frowned, feeling defeated. She nodded. She turned to her people.

As they stood in front of Bell House, the yellow eye illuminated their scared faces.

"Listen to me, people of Letfreedomring. It seems for the time being, we are these men's prisoners. I'm sorry I let you down. It may appear as if all hope is lost, but have faith. We will find a way to defeat these evil men. For now, I need you to do as they say."

The people of Letfreedomring wailed and cried and peered around in fear as the men of Nork prodded them into movement. Moxies looked around for something, making Restaria curious.

"Many of these people are weak, with scrabblers and elders," Restaria pleaded. "They will never make a long journey!"

Moxie ignored her. "Where'd I leave my chopper?" Moxie looked upset and disappointed, and he tried to remember, but at the time he left it, he wasn't thinking. "Nuts. Well, ain't got time to look for it now. I'll just have to come back later on my own. There ain't gonna be anyone here to steal it, that's for sure."

He turned to Restaria again. "You ain't gotta worry. Being the boss lady, I'll make sure you have a ride. But the rest better just put on their walking shoes and get ready for a long stroll."

Just then, Clancy rode up, carrying a struggling Deb in front of him. Moxie stopped and turned with a big grin on his face.

"Well, well, what do we have here, Clancy?" Moxie asked.

"A bonnie lass I found wandering in the city like a lost sheep. And a fighting tiger she is too. I have a ken for her. You give her to me, we'll call ourselves even."

Restaria looked at Deb, even more unhappiness showing on her face.

"Ain't nobody dividin' up spoils until we get back to Nork," Moxie said. "In fact, I think she oughta ride with me for, uh, safe keeping." He chuckled darkly. 'The rest, let's get a move on. I'm itching to get out of here before those monsters show up again."

As Clancy watched with disappointment Deb climbed off his rat-beastie and climbed on another one Moxie had found for himself. As she left Clancy she glared at him one more time, and he grinned back with humor and desire.

Once again, they all started forward, the Norkers and the people of Letfreedomring hurrying, for neither wanted to face the Krakn again.

It wasn't long before they left Bell House far behind and wove their way down the deserted streets of Pelpia.

Super and Lightpole stood behind a stone column on the porch of a brick building, trying to stay out of sight. They watched helpless as Moxie and the Norkers herded the people of Letfreedomring away.

"It appears all is lost," Lightpole said, his voice full of defeat.

"You sure are defeatist," Super said irritably. "Have a little faith, will ya?"

"Faith in what?" Lightpole said with anger. "Our army is defeated. The Norkers are taking my people away to slavery. We cannot fight them alone. Just what do you suggest?"

Super rolled her eyes. "Why did they put a Gloomy Gus like you in charge of the army?"

"I don't know what a Gloomy Gus is," Lightpole said. "You people are always talking strange things."

Super grinned in the darkness. "We learned them from Misterwizard. I wish he was here now. He'd know what to do."

That gave her an idea.

"I know what we're going to do!"

"What?" Lightpole said, curious despite himself.

"We're going to find you some allies!"

"Allies?"

"That's right. Hey, you got any way to get around, transportation?"

"We had a few horse-beasties, but they are surely scattered or eaten by now," Lightpole replied.

"You're so much help. We're just going to have to find one. There's no way we can get to New Sanctuary on foot, not before it's way too late."

"The horse-beasties were kept in a building behind Bell House. There may be some there still."

"It looks like they're gone. I think it's safe for us to come out. Lead the way, Mcduff," Super said.

Lightpole shook his head, a strong look of disapproval on his face at having to endure more of her strange words.

They walked to Bell House and were about to pass by it, when Super saw something way better than a horse-beastie. She ran over to it with a look of pure joy.

"Hey, there's a Harley here!"

She stood it up and climbed on. As Lightpole watched with intense curiosity, she looked at him.

"Cross your fingers."

"Stop saying things like that!' Lightpole said grumpily.

Super turned the switch and started the Harley. A wonderful and welcome rumbling came from the engine.

"Yahoo!" Super yelled. "Climb on. We've got a long way to go, and a short time to get there."

"Is this contraption safe?" Lightpole said as he gingerly climbed on behind her. "And are you sure you know how to ride it?"

"Don't you worry about that. I'm a Biker Babe, taught by my man to ride. Hold on to your hat!"

Super sped off and Lightpole yelped, grabbing onto her for dear life.

They sped off into the darkness, heading for New Sanctuary, seemingly a million miles away.

Johnny and Starbucks sped towards Bell House, down the dark, dirty street, past the wrecked buildings on either side. Having ridden a lot now, they rode confidently, used to weaving around the old rusted cars and plants that had grown up in the street. They still had to be careful for where vegetation had covered the street it could be slippery, so they kept their mind on how the tires gripped the road, ready to slow down if they felt them slipping.

Johnny thought about Deb. There was so much going on, so many dangers. He never should have left her. But when he did, everything seemed safe and stable. Now, he had no idea where she was, or what danger she was in. The thought of anything happening to her filled him with dread. He knew that if she were harmed, he would never be able to forgive himself.

Johnny looked over at Starbucks. His black skin made him harder to see at night, just a dark shadow on a

Harley whose chrome shone from the light of the yellow eye. Johnny saw that Starbucks looked worried too. He was sure Starbucks was thinking about Super just like he was about Deb. Super was wounded as well. They had to hurry.

Johnny sped up, heedless of the possibility of slipping, and Starbucks quickly mimicked him. They sped past old windowless buildings, their interiors blackness. Johnny kept a wary eye for more Krakn or Nord soldiers. They didn't need to get caught up in another battle. They had to get to Deb and Super.

They grew close to Bell House and could see it in the distance. They ringing sound had stopped. Johnny's inside tightened, wondering if they were too late for whatever happened.

"Nobody's here, Johnny!" Starbucks yelled as they rode up to the building. The surrounding landscape was silent as a tomb, and it gave Johnny the chills.

"I wonder if they all went south, back towards Sanctuary."

"How will we know which way to go?" Starbucks said, as they sat on their Harleys idling.

From the darkness, a small group of figures emerged. They were short and slight, and Johnny and Starbucks could tell they were scrabblers. They came from Johnny and Starbuck's right, walking in what almost looked like formation. In the front, one scrabbler seemed to be leading them.

"Now what?" Starbucks said.

Johnny grinned. "This is the night for weird surprises."

The scrabblers, lead by the one in front, walked up until they were close enough to talk to Johnny and Starbucks.

"You're Johnny Apocalypse," the lead boy said, his eyes twinkling with excitement.

"That's right," Johnny replied. "Who are you, and who are these scrabblers?"

The boy puffed his chest out, and it was apparent he was proud to be in charge. "I am Redeye. And we don't like being called scrabblers."

Johnny and Starbucks chuckled. "Sorry, no offense," Johnny said.

"We just came from hiding. But it looks like we're on our own for now."

"Why do you say that?" Starbucks asked.

"Didn't you see?" Redeye replied. "We did. We was watching from a building over there. The Norkers took our whole city captive. They're taking them to Nork to be slaves."

Johnny and Starbucks reacted with shock and dismay.

"Was there a young lady with them with blond hair?"

Redeye nodded. "They made a big fuss over her. They were fighting over her."

Starbucks said with worry, "What about a girl with long black hair and an attitude?"

"You mean Super?" Redeye said. "We met her. She left us in the big building with the lions while she helped Lightpole. I don't know if she was captured or not."

Johnny and Starbucks looked at each other with concern, wondering just what to do next.

"Did they capture your mayr, Restaria?" Redeye nodded. "They sure did. They sat her on one of their rat-beasties and she rode off with them."

Johnny and Starbucks just sat for a moment, thinking. Then Johnny said, "Are you scrabb- I mean children going to be okay on your own?"

Redeye puffed himself up again with pride. "I can take care of them. I am used to being in charge."

"Good," Johnny said, looking at him. "Look, I'm sure they didn't get everyone. You need to hide, until some more people of your army show up."

"I got it," Redeye said. "And if they don't, we'll just make a new society of our own!"

Johnny and Starbucks grinned. Then they looked

at each other for a moment.

"What do you think, Johnny?" Starbucks asked.

"I know I have to go after Deb," Johnny replied. "I'm not sure what you should do, Starbucks."

"I don't know either. I could search the whole city looking for Super, and she might be captured and on her way to Nork the whole time."

"Why don't you wait here for a little while and see if she shows up. Meanwhile, I'll head after the Nork army. If she doesn't, you can ride up to join me."

"Okay," Starbucks said, but he didn't sound confident.

CHAPTER 28

The Nork army and the captives of Letfreedomring passed through the north gate and left the walls of Pelpia behind. Then they wove their way down the car choked ribbon of gray, on their way to Nork. The people were slow, having women and scrabblers and old folks amongst them. Everyone, including the Norkers, kept a wary eye around them, hoping they wouldn't run into any more Krakn.

From the back of the ratty she rode in front of Moxie, Deb turned and peered into the darkness behind her. The city looked empty and forlorn, but she still she felt a strong desire to go back to it.

"Johnny! Johnny!"

Moxie chuckled. "Who's this Johnny fella you're going on about? Do I got another rooster in the hen house?"

Deb turned her head and glared at him. "He's my mate, and he's the one who's going to put a sword through your heart. If you're smart, you'll let me go now, or he's going to kill you."

Moxie grinned and his eyes twinkled. "That's the second joker who said he's gonna kill me today. Let him come, sweetheart. I love a good fight."

"He's the one who turned the Krakn on you, I'll bet," Deb said, smiling with grim satisfaction.

"Then he's definitely a mug I want to meet. I owe him, big time."

Restaria, who rode next to Deb on a rat-beastie by herself, said, "Don't worry, Deb. Johnny will come for you!"

"For both of us!" Deb yelled back. She knew Johnny would come, all right. She just didn't want him to. She didn't want him risking his life for her, and there was little chance he'd be able to find her once they reached Nork. It was up to her to get free, and help Restaria free her people. No matter what happened, she was going to prove to Johnny that she could be just as brave and fierce as he was.

She gazed behind them one more time, and she was sure she saw a lone figure on a Harley, far in the distance, following them. Or was it just her desire making her imagination run wild? Only time would tell.

On they traveled, heading towards new uncertainties and dangers.

Deecee loped along, sniffing the ground, looking for anything tasty to eat. There was nothing around, just moldy vegetation, rusted cars and empty buildings. Nothing really seemed interesting at all. But experience told him he might see a beastie at any moment, and then he'd have a merry chase and maybe even a tasty meal.

He stopped and looked up. He realized he'd made a mistake running off and leaving his master's friend behind. He didn't feel the loyalty to her he felt for his master, but knew he knew she was his master's mate, and he did like her a lot. He knew he should obey her too, just because it made his master happy. He sensed he'd been bad by running off. Now he was all alone, and hungry.

He raised his nose and sniffed at the air for anything familiar, something to give him an idea of which way to turn. His black fur moved from the wind, and he straightened his pointed ears up, listening. There was nothing but the soft whisper of the wind. Deecee decided he should head back to where he'd seen his master's mate before. Hopefully from there at least he could pick up her trail again.

As he turned and headed back, he kept his ears open for any enemies, as he always did. It wouldn't do to be caught unawares. An enemy would wait in the dark and spring at the last moment, and unless he was ready, he would have the disadvantage. Before he met his master he'd been on his own, and had many fights. Most were with other barkers, but a few were with big cat-beasties, or bear-beasties, or even other strange creatures like one that was white and black with a long nose and long claws that for its small size was fierce. That one almost finished him and Deecee had to run away and nurse his wounds. He wouldn't try to tangle with one of those again.

He'd also attacked other beasties himself, mostly for food, including taking down a deer-beastie all on his own. He'd chased it for miles, but finally when it was too tired to run anymore, he was able to jump on it and bite its throat. Somehow at the time, killing and eating the deer-beastie woke something deep inside Deecee, a feeling of savagery that made Deecee feel like a wild beastie. That was the best meal Deecee remembered, and he cherished the feeling it gave him of being free and terrible, feared by all other beasties. Then he found his new master, and all those feelings seem to fade again. He loved his new master, and would do anything for him. It was wonderful having someone to serve and get affection in return.

For in reality, Deecee was never a wild beastie. He had another master a long time ago, an older master who treated him well and fed him whatever he ate. The master used to lie next to Deecee and stroke his fur at night and talk to him. They lived in a small one-story building on the outskirts of town that said, "Joe's Tavern" on the outside, though Deecee had no way of knowing that. His old master had laid blankets on the floor behind a curved table that was right in the middle of the room. His master used to drink from dusty old bottles lining a shelf and sing to himself, clutching the bottle to his bosom and laying on the blankets next to Deecee.

Then one day, his old master said, "Stary here, Whiskey. I'm going out to find us some food." Then he went out clutching a bottle to his chest. He never returned. Deecee waited for a long time, for two cycles of the yellow eye, until he was so hungry, he couldn't wait any longer. Then reluctantly he trotted out, looking for some his master, or something to eat.

He was on his own for a long time, hiding in the shadows whenever danger appeared, drinking from stale pools of water and hunting raccoon-beasties and squirrel-beasties for his food. Occasionally he would catch a rabbit-beastie as well.

Now he had a new master, and he didn't want to lose him too. His master had been gone for a long time, and Deecee had no idea where he went. He had stayed with his master's mate like he was told until he grew hungry and decided once again, he had to go looking for his own food. Now he was all alone. He wondered if once again, he was going to be on his own. The thought made Deecee sad, for he really liked his new master, and he liked having someone to take care of him and not have to fight for his own survival.

Deecee trotted faster, hoping he could find his way back to his master's mate before they too disappeared.

Suddenly Deecee saw something move in the darkness to his left. He stopped and backed up, sniffing the air. The night was lit by the yellow eye, and Deecee could see well at night.

It was black, and had many legs and arms, and it moved them silently in the darkness. Deecee didn't need anyone to tell him that this was a bad beastie to be avoided. It was much bigger than Deecee, and he knew there was no way he could fight and kill it in a battle.

Deecee slowly backed up, keeping as silent as he could. The beastie worked on something, and as Deecee watched, it lifted a piece of something up in the air and moved it towards its mouth. Deecee realized it was part of a master, its head. This creature was eating someone.

Deecee continued to back up until he as far enough away that he could turn and run, but at the last moment the thing turned and saw him. It screeched and took off after Deecee, running like lightning on its four legs.

Deecee didn't waste any time running away as fast as he could. He ran down the street as fast as he could, looking for a place to hide. The beastie screeched behind him and Deecee put every ounce of energy into running.

To his right across the street stood a tall building. It's yawning black opening beckoned to him. Deecee ran across the street and inside and peered around in the dark, panting. The dark interior was filled with old desks and shelves, all covered with mold. The room ran back quite a way, and Deecee was sure he could find a place to hide. He ran inside quickly and loped towards the back of the building.

And just in time, for no sooner had Deecee ran down the floor than the dark shape of the beastie filled the doorway. *It must have seen him run inside*, Deecee thought, as he whined with fear and tried to find a place to hide

There was an open doorway to the right, and Deecee could see stairs inside. He decided it would be too much of a trap. He saw a long hallway with doorways leading into small rooms, but they all had only one way in. If he went into them, he'd be easy prey.

Deecee decided his only hope was to hide long enough for the beastie to get far inside, then run out past it again and away before it could follow.

He silently padded to a corner of the big room in the front and lay down behind a big steel box that lay on the floor. Then, with only his eyes over the top of the box, he watched the doorway and the beastie.

It came in slowly, as if sensing a trap, and peered around in the darkness. Its long arms touched things as it passed, as if it could get a sense of what they were by the touch.

It stopped when it was ten feet into the room and just waited, listening. It was blocking the exit! Deecee had to be as quiet as he could, hoping it was not hear him.

They stayed like that for what felt like an eternity to Deecee, as his heart pounded with fear. Deecee watched the beastie intently, not moving a muscle. Then it moved towards him!

Deecee figured it must have spotted him. He had no choice but to fight. As the beastie grew close, Deecee sprang. With a savage growl, he bit one of the beastie's legs and crunched down hard. The beastie screeched and waved its arm around, but Deecee held on.

It flung Deecee through the air, but Deecee didn't let go. Finally, the beastie managed to shake Deecee free. Deecee flew through the air and landed on the dirty tile covered floor, rolling over and over. He leapt up and snarled, ready to fight.

The beastie bled from the bite mark where Deecee bit him. It nursed the wound with one of its arms and stared at Deecee. With pleasure, Deecee realized it was scared of him now.

Grinning and panting, Deecee took off and ran outside again, happy to have won the fight and survived to fight another day. Behind him in the doorway the creature came out, but slowly, as if happy with letting Deecee put some distance between them.

Deecee continued to run silently and swiftly through the darkness. Then he heard something that didn't fill him with dread, but joy. It was the sound of a Harley machine! Could it be his master?

Deecee quickly ran towards the sound. He ran onto a major street lined with cars and stopped. He peered around, trying to hear which direction the sound came from.

And then he saw it, far in the distance. It was his

master, riding away! Happiness filled Deecee's heart, but also a feeling of panic. He ran as fast as he could towards his master, hoping he could catch up to him before his master got too far away.

He ran on, panting with exertion, through the dark night, away from a city that now seemed silent and empty, but was full of life, and danger.